Iain Dalgleish

THE UPS AND DOWNS OF
NORMAN DRUDGE

Published in the United Kingdom by Amazon in 2020.

Copyright © 2020 by Iain Dalgleish.

Iain Dalgleish has asserted his right under the Copyright, Designs and Patents Act 1988 to be identified as the author of this work.

First published in Great Britain in 2020 by Amazon.

ISBN 9798635829066

Iain Dalgleish can be contacted at:
iaindalgleishauthor@gmail.com

THE UPS AND DOWNS OF

NORMAN DRUDGE

Chapter One

I'd see him there, on most days, sat in his window, looking out towards the street. He was either drinking tea, eating biscuits or looking through his binoculars. He was an elderly man, well, elderly to me anyway. Someone said that he was in the civil service, or some sort of office worker. His name was Norman, Nigel, Howard or some such name. I knew very little about him, we had certainly never talked, never exchanged pleasantries. I'd seen him once in the street when walking back from the tube station. I looked his way but our eyes never met. He just kept his head down and walked straight ahead, quickly up his steps and straight through his front door as fast as he could. Once I was back indoors, I looked across to his window and there he was again, staring out towards the street, drinking a cup of tea and eating a biscuit.

It was a Thursday morning. The dustbin men were in the street with their noisy vehicles and their incessant beeps. It was recycling week. Every other week was recycling week when all our old plastic bottles, jam jars and cardboard were collected. The street was at its noisiest when the dustbin men were around, second only to our horse-faced, overly-tattooed, bald postman who insisted on slamming gates and banging on doors as loudly as possible.

'He could wake the dead, Gemma,' said Mrs Dawson as she drank a cup of tea at my kitchen table.

Mrs Dawson liked her tea made with proper tea, no teabags, and brewed in a teapot. The pot had to be warmed first and the tea had to be allowed to settle before it was poured into a china cup. A dash of milk, poured from a milk jug not a plastic bottle, and all was right with the world.

'I could never drink tea from a builder's mug,' said Mrs Dawson. The thought of drinking tea from a mug, 'a builder's mug' as she called it, sent her face into a strange contortion.

And so it was every Thursday, whenever the dustbin men were about, Mrs Dawson would come over and we'd drink tea and put the world to rights.

'Have you got a biscuit, love?' she'd always ask, but would only eat Rich Tea which she nibbled carefully so as to not get any crumbs anywhere. She most certainly wasn't a dunker.

I liked my tea with a teabag, in a mug, and happily dunked biscuits even if part of them fell into the cup. However, on a Thursday, I kept up the charade and drank my tea, like Mrs Dawson, from a china cup.

'What do you think of that man across the way?' asked Mrs Dawson.

'Norman?' I said.

'Is that his name?' she asked.

'I don't know,' I replied. 'He just looks like a Norman to me.'

'Well, him,' she said, nodding in the general direction of Norman's house.

'He just sits there all day, drinking tea and eating biscuits,' she continued, failing to see the irony. 'And always from a builder's mug.'

I smiled.

'I suppose he's not doing anyone any harm,' I said.

'But he's always watching, looking through those binoculars of his,' said Mrs Dawson.

'I believe he's some sort of office worker,' I said.

'I don't know how,' replied Mrs Dawson. 'He never moves.'

It went quiet for a minute as we drank our tea and Mrs Dawson slowly nibbled her biscuit.

'I see the woman at number 16 has got a new dog,' she announced, breaking the silence. 'A right yappy thing it is. It's one of those little dogs that daft girls carry around in their handbags.'

'A Chihuahua?' I suggested.

'I don't know,' replied Mrs Dawson. 'It's one of those yappy ones anyway.'

Mrs Dawson had been coming around for tea every Thursday morning for the last couple of years since her husband Alf had died of a heart attack. He'd worked for the local council, catching rats and such like. They'd given him a brass carriage clock when he retired which ticked away on Mrs Dawson's mantlepiece. Mrs Dawson wasn't keen on it. It ran on a battery not like in her day when all clocks had to be wound with a special key. Anyway, she kept it, sitting pride of place on the mantle piece, ticking away, because it reminded her of 'my Alf', as she called him.

Mrs Dawson's first name was Doreen, not that I would have ever dreamed of calling her Doreen, she was always Mrs Dawson to me. She was well into her seventies although she would never discuss her age.

'You're as old as you feel,' she'd say often.

We'd met in the local charity shop where I worked on a Saturday. I'd seen her there many times before I got to know her, always looking at the knick-knack section. Mrs Walters was in charge of the knick-knack display which included donated vases, ornaments and pottery animals. Wooden deer, the sort that were common in the 1960s and 1970s, seemed very popular recently.

'I don't suppose you've got one of those Siamese cats,' Mrs Dawson said to me one particular Saturday. 'You know, the one where it's peering at a mouse in a wine class.'

'I could look in the back room,' I said. The back room was the place where recently-donated items lay until they were sorted out and put onto the shelves. Some of it never made it to the shop, either too tatty or just too smelly to do anything with.

'We've nothing like that,' shouted across Mrs Walters, who had overheard our conversation. 'I know the ones you mean, my sister had one sat on her front window ledge for many years.'
Mrs Dawson smiled over to her.

'That was a very long time ago though,' Mrs Walters continued. 'Back in the 1970s and our Karen has been gone for many years now.'

Mrs Walters was always talking about her sister 'our Karen' who had died of breast cancer some time back in the 1980s.

'We'll never get over it,' she'd say often and

sometimes disappear into the back room when she was feeling tearful.

So that's how my friendship with Mrs Dawson began, all over a Siamese cat looking over a wine glass at a mouse.

'My husband Alf and me had one when we first married,' she said. 'He died recently. I do miss him even though he could be very annoying at times.'

Somehow we got talking, she remembered many of the same things my mother remembered, old television programmes, singers, the Black and White Minstrels and the like. Old television comedies where people could be as unpolitical as they liked and everyone laughed. She particularly liked Benny Hill.

'Don't get me wrong, I'm not racist,' she said. 'I just liked things how they used to be. I miss shows like the Black and White Minstrels, I did like Dai Francis.'

As we talked, I told Mrs Dawson about myself. She seemed to have a knack of gleaning information from strangers. I told her my age, twenty-five, and how I lived alone in a flat at Winslow Place. Mrs Dawson, by coincidence, it turned out, lived in the same street. We had never seen each other or passed as far as I knew. I told her how I worked at the library most days of the week apart from Thursdays which were my day off, not that I got up to much, just wandering around the local park and perhaps, if it was sunny, feeding the ducks a few scraps of bread, even though there was a sign saying not to. White bread, apparently, was bad for them although they seemed quite happy with it as far as I could tell. I could see that, like myself, Mrs Dawson was feeling lonely. It was a big city and making new friends was pretty difficult, so I invited her around to my flat one Thursday morning for a cup of tea and a chat about the 'old days'. That was two years ago.

'I see that number 46 has got a new car,' said Mrs Dawson. 'It's a huge thing, more like a lorry. She only uses it to take her children to school in the morning. Her husband's a surly character, bald head and tattoos, never speaks.'

I'd seen the Andersons' new 4x4, all chrome with four spotlights along the top in case they needed to go out hunting any night of the week although what sort of wildlife they were going to find in Ealing was anyone's guess.

'They have a son called Keanu,' I said. 'And a daughter called Beyoncé.'

Mrs Dawson sighed.

'Children have such strange names nowadays,' she said.

I moved my cup and saucer to one side so that I didn't knock it with my elbow. I could be very clumsy at times.

'I think her husband's a plumber,' I said. 'He's got a white van with 'Darren's Plumbing' on the side.'

Mrs Dawson looked down towards the street to see if she could see it but Darren was out on a job, £90 an hour apparently. Mr Peters at the library had once called him out after a pipe at his home had sprung a leak.

'Three hundred and fifty pounds,' he'd said at the time. 'Can you believe it?'

And he had to get him back twice more after it continued to leak.

'I fixed it myself in the end,' continued Mr Peters. 'Never again.'

'Alf had a Morris Traveller,' announced Mrs

Dawson as she reached for another Rich Tea to nibble away at. 'Is there any more tea?'
I poured her another cup.

'I hope it's not stewed,' I said.

'It'll be fine, dear,' she replied.

She gazed out of the window for a couple of seconds across to the Bradshaw's. Mr Bradshaw was something in the city, an accountant Mrs Bishop had said. I'd seen him on the tube, smartly dressed in a suit carrying a foldaway umbrella.

'He loved that car,' continued Mrs Dawson. 'We went everywhere in it. Scotland I remember one time, all those men in kilts, playing bagpipes. I loved trips to the seaside. We even went to Butlin's one year. I suppose it was about 1973. When was Edward Heath Prime Minister?'

I had no idea although my mum said that my great gran did a wonderful impression of him, chuckling and shrugging her shoulders up and down. Actually, I think that gran was doing an impression of Mike Yarwood doing Edward Heath.

'I don't know,' I replied. 'The early 1970s perhaps?'

'Well, it must have been 1973,' continued Mrs Dawson. 'The Saint had just become James Bond.'

'The Saint?' I inquired.

'You know, The Saint,' said Mrs Dawson. 'Roger Moore. Alf took me to see Live and Let Die at the Odeon.'

'Was it good?' I asked.

'I'm not sure I liked it very much,' she replied. 'It was all voodoo, platform shoes and crocodiles. Oh, and a large unpleasant man with a false arm.'

I think that I'd seen the film on the television one rainy

autumn afternoon when there hadn't been much else to do.

'Alf and I preferred Sean Connery,' said Mrs Dawson. 'And then there was the other one, George something or other.'

'George Clooney?' I suggested.

'No, not him,' said Mrs Dawson. 'It was way back, the 1960s anyway.'

'Was he any good?' I asked.

'He was alright,' she replied. 'He married Diana Rigg but then she was shot by Kojak, you know that bald actor. It was awfully sad.'

'I'll look out for it,' I said, slightly confused by the conversation.

'I think that Alf would have liked to have been more like James Bond,' said Mrs Dawson. 'Although I couldn't imagine the secret service employing a rat catcher.'
She smiled.

'It must have been 1973,' she continued. 'Everyone was wearing platform shoes and flared trousers. Alf had a pair for a while.'

'Flared trousers?' I inquired.

'No, well, yes,' replied Mrs Dawson. 'He had flared trousers but also had a pair of platform shoes.'

'Oh,' I said.

'For a while he was six foot four,' she said, 'but he couldn't get on with them. They made him look like Frankenstein, clonking around everywhere. He sprained his ankle more than once.'

'It's funny how fashions change,' I said while imagining Alf in his glam rock get up. I'd only ever seen him in a photograph on Mrs Dawson's mantlepiece wearing a tweed jacket and smoking a pipe. He didn't look like he'd ever been into fashion.

'Yes, it was 1973. Slade, Wizzard and Roxy Music were on Top of the Pops,' said Mrs Dawson, 'and that man who's always in trouble with the police.' I assumed that she meant Gary Glitter but I didn't want to mention his name out loud. Perhaps she meant Rolf Harris or the other one. Mrs Dawson always referred to him as the 'other one' as if mentioning his name would somehow conjure him up.

'Shall I make a fresh pot of tea?' I asked, noticing that Mrs Dawson's last over-stewed cup of tea had been left half-drunk.

'That would be lovely, dear,' she replied. 'I do like these biscuits, where do you get them from?' She looked the packet up and down.

'Just the local shop,' I replied. 'On the corner, Mr Patel's.'

'Oh,' said Mrs Dawson. 'I remember when Mr Noble owned the shop. It was a long time ago now. He sold broken biscuits and you could buy half a loaf if you wanted.'
The thought of broken biscuits didn't sound appealing. Mr Patel's unbroken biscuits sounded a much better deal even if they were sometimes well past their sell-by date.

'No, no,' continued Mrs Dawson. 'I wouldn't shop in Patel's. I once bought Alf a packet of Shreddies in there and the competition on the back had closed three years previously.'

'You can get Rich Tea biscuits in any shop,' I said. 'Lidl's in the high street has them.'

'It was a competition to win a holiday to Florida,' said Mrs Dawson. 'Three years out of date, can you imagine?'

I smiled.

'Heaven knows how long he'd had the Shreddies in the shop,' she continued. 'Not that Alf would have gone to Florida anyway. He hated flying.' Mrs Dawson lifted her china cup to her lips and blew lightly on her tea before taking a sip.

'Perfect,' she said.

'Alf wouldn't have liked Florida,' said Mrs Dawson. 'Far too hot and full of crocodiles.'

'I think they're alligators,' I replied. Mrs Dawson took another sip of tea.

'Is there a difference?' she inquired.

'A difference?' I asked.

'Between crocodiles and alligators,' she replied.

'I think that alligators are from America and crocodiles are from Africa,' I said.

'Oh,' she replied, taking another sip of tea. 'Alf wouldn't have liked either.' Norman sat down in his window with a cup of tea and picked up his binoculars. He stared intently across the street.

'I wonder what he's looking at?' said Mrs Dawson.

'Birds, probably,' I said, although the only wildlife in the area seemed to be a few sparrows, a pigeon and an occasional squirrel. Mr Parsons had a bird feeder but it attracted rats and the council had asked him to take it down.

'More likely that young girl's large chest at number 10,' said Mrs Dawson. 'She sunbathes topless in the back garden sometimes. I wouldn't be surprised if she gets backache when she's older.' We both contemplated the lady at number 10 and her large chest.

'I think he's just watching the birds,' I said again.

Mrs Dawson changed the subject.

'Our Sally's decided to become a vegetarian,' she said. 'It's all soya beans and tofu. I couldn't be doing with all that.'

'I thought of becoming a vegetarian,' I said.

'I wouldn't like to try it,' said Mrs Dawson. 'It's so unappetising. I hate to think what Alf would have made of soya beans for his Sunday dinner. And he did like a bacon sandwich.'

The talk of a bacon sandwich made me feel hungry. I had no bacon in the house, I would have to pop out to Mr Patel's later.

Mrs Dawson placed her china cup back in its saucer and sighed.

'It's meant to rain later,' she said. 'And I've so much shopping to do.'

'Mr Patel's is convenient,' I said. 'It's just on the corner.'

'Oh, no, that won't do,' she replied. 'I'll get on the bus and go to Tesco, they've got everything I want.'

With that Mrs Dawson got to her feet and put on her coat. It was one of those tartan affairs with a fur-lined collar. Alf had bought it for her many years before.

'I see Norman is still there,' she said nodding towards his bay window.

We both looked out of the window and stared. For a split second, our eyes and Norman's met but he soon looked away. He picked up his paper, it looked like the Mail, and started to read it, shaking it slightly so that all the pages fell into place neatly.

'Oh well, love,' said Mrs Dawson. 'Thanks for the tea. I do enjoy our Thursday morning chats.

Perhaps I'll see you at the park later?'

'I'll be there at about two,' I said.

'It's a date,' said Mrs Dawson, smiling. 'Oh, and bring some bread. The ducks do enjoy some bread but not that cheap stuff from Patel's. Even I couldn't eat that.'

I walked to the door and let Mrs Dawson out, waving as she headed towards the bus stop for her trip to Tesco. The number 29 came every quarter of an hour and would drop her off right at the entrance.

Chapter Two

The park was unusually quiet. I put it down to another closing down sale at a large shop in the town. It sold trainers and other 'sports gear' such as those nylon pants with a stripe down both sides. Everyone wanted a bargain, it seemed. Its customers didn't look particularly sporty, overweight people looking for jogging pants which stretched easy and had a lot of give in them.

The ducks quacked in anticipation. There were quite a few of them today. Mainly just the ordinary ones and one stray Mandarin duck which had appeared in the park two summers' previously. It mostly kept itself to itself. We'd had a black swan for a while but it didn't seem to get on with the white ones and left. I hadn't heeded Mrs Dawson's advice and had bought a cheap loaf from Mr Patel's. I liked Mr Patel, always friendly and polite and he always opened the door for me. Who cared if some products were slightly out of date? They were edible, weren't they?

Mr Patel's whole family seemed to work in the

shop including his nephew, Sanjay. Sanjay was always courteous to customers even to Mrs Robinson who had spent some time in the 1960s in the Far East with her naval commander husband. She talked down to all of the Patels but they never let her rudeness bother them. Mrs Robinson behaved as if Britain still had an empire and Indian people were there to run around after her. Mr Patel was never impolite to her although he drew the line when she tried bartering with him. Mrs Dawson said that she thought that Mrs Robinson had a touch of Alzheimer's.

'They'll take over one day,' Mrs Robinson said often. 'We'll all be killed in our beds.'

I'd seen the whole Patel family, at one time or another, apart from Mrs Patel. In fact, there appeared to be no Mrs Patel. Perhaps she'd died. I didn't like to ask.

Although Mr Patel had an Indian accent, he was very well spoken. His father also worked in the shop and often served customers, always wearing a brown knitted tank top. Someone said that he'd learned how to speak English from the BBC World Service.

'Is one off to the park?' asked Mr Patel Senior, as I handed over 59p for the loaf of bread.

'It is good weather for ducks,' he joked, missing the whole point of the saying.

'I'm meeting Mrs Dawson,' I said.

'Yes, Mrs Dawson,' replied Mr Patel Senior, uncertain as to who Mrs Dawson was.

'She lives at number 29,' I said.

'Oh, yes,' replied Mr Patel Senior, handing me the bread.

'Have a nice day,' he said as I made my way to the exit.

'And you,' I replied.

The ducks seemed particularly aggressive today. One blue and grey one kept trying to jump on the brown ones' backs, pulling violently at their feathers.

'I think they're probably mating,' said Mrs Dawson as she sat down beside me. 'My Alf used to be like that at one time.'

She smiled at me and winked. I smiled back but didn't dwell too long on Mr and Mrs Dawson's love life.

'Did you get your shopping?' I asked.

'Oh, yes,' replied Mrs Dawson. 'Carrots seem particularly expensive nowadays, don't they?'
I hadn't noticed.

'That man was on the bus again,' said Mrs Dawson. 'You know, the one with the wild ginger hair and the grey zip up flying suit.'
I knew who she meant. The regulars on the bus called him 'Emo' for some unknown reason.

'He was going up and down the aisles saying 'tickets please' to everyone,' said Mrs Dawson. 'He can be very annoying at times.'

'I think that he has mental health issues,' I said.

'He's a bit simple,' said Mrs Dawson. 'His father was just the same, running up and down the common, machine gunning flies.'

'I don't remember his father,' I said.

'It was before your time, dear,' said Mrs Dawson.
She picked up the loaf of bread I'd bought and gave it a shake.

'Hmm,' she said. 'Is this from Patel's?'

'The ducks like it,' I replied as they gathered impatiently around our feet, quacking loudly.

Mrs Dawson opened it up, broke a bit off and then broke it into smaller pieces before sprinkling it in front of the ducks. It was soon gone and she took out some more and repeated the process.

'I saw Norman Drudge in Tesco,' she said.

'Who?' I asked.

'Norman Drudge,' she replied. 'The man with the cup of tea and binoculars who lives opposite.'
I wondered if I'd missed something. Was he really called 'Norman Drudge'?

'Well, that's what I call him,' continued Mrs Dawson. 'He looks like a Norman, doesn't he, and Drudge seems as good a surname as any and seems to suit him.'

'Did he see you?' I asked.

'I don't think so,' replied Mrs Dawson, 'although I was standing practically beside him.'

'Could you see what he was buying?' I inquired.
I realised that it sounded nosy but I somehow felt that if I knew what he ate I would somehow learn more about Norman.

'One of those meals for one,' Mrs Dawson replied. 'Like that meerkat in the advert that's shown just before Coronation Street.'
Mrs Dawson did her impression of the meerkat on the advert saying 'Meal for one' in her best Romanian-type accent. It was really quite good and we both smiled.

'I saw him again in the queue,' she said. 'Just a box of teabags, a packet of digestives and his meal for one. The lady in front of me let him go first.'

'Oh,' I said. 'What does he talk like?'

'Just an average sort of voice,' Mrs Dawson replied. 'He hardly said much.'

So all we knew of Norman was that he liked tea, ate digestives, bought meals for one and, in many ways, was just an average person who would go unnoticed in most situations. We only noticed him because he lived across the street.

The ducks gathered aggressively at our feet, quacking and pecking hard at the ground for any missed crumbs.

'They really are quite hungry,' said Mrs Dawson, breaking off more bread for the ducks. The duck that had earlier been attacking the female ducks was now fighting for prime position to get as much food as possible.

'He's quite a plucky character,' said Mrs Dawson. 'He doesn't want the others to have any.' She laughed as she tried to shoo him away.

'How much did you pay for this bread?' she asked.

'59p,' I replied. 'From Patel's.'

'I hope it doesn't make them ill,' said Mrs Dawson, looking disgruntled.

'It's no different from any other bread,' I said. Mrs Dawson looked the packet up and down again.

'I wouldn't like to eat it,' she said.

'It makes lovely toast,' I said. 'It's nice with marmalade.'

'Even so,' said Mrs Dawson. 'I don't think my Alf would have eaten it.'

We broke up the rest of the bread into small pieces before feeding it to the ducks. Mrs Dawson made sure that it was equally distributed and that the aggressive duck wasn't getting more than his fair share.

'How's work?' she asked.

'Just the same as usual,' I replied. 'I had a man come in the other day and ask for The Kama Sutra.'

'How odd,' said Mrs Dawson. 'Does the library stock it?'

'Oh, yes,' I replied. 'We have several copies but I had to wait while Mr Peters checked to see if he could locate one.

'Is he the man with the ornate moustache?' asked Mrs Dawson.

'Yes,' I replied. 'I don't think any of the customers ever call him Mr Peters, they just call him 'the man with the moustache'.

Mr Peters' moustache was legendary in library circles. It was a Jimmy Edwards-type affair with the ends knitted in cat tails so they drooped down towards his chin.

Mr Peters knew the library inside out. He knew where every book was kept just by a mention of its title. He'd been at the library for as long as anyone could remember but all I knew about him was that he had a cat called Malcolm. There were endless photos of Malcolm on Mr Peters' phone.

The ducks dispersed as we ran out of bread and returned to the pond awaiting their next supplier of food.

'We've a meeting at the library tomorrow morning,' I said. 'I've got to get in early.'

'What's it about?' asked Mrs Dawson.

'I'm not sure,' I replied. 'A stock-take, perhaps. I don't mind going in early, I like Fridays. People seem happier. I suppose it's because the weekend is coming.'

We stared out across the pond. A man in tight blue Lycra was doing star jumps on the far bank before touching his toes and running quickly on the spot.

'Alf loved the weekends,' said Mrs Dawson. 'He would stay in bed until 9am on Saturdays, I'd make him a cooked breakfast and, if it was sunny, he'd sit in the garden reading the newspaper until dinnertime. At 11am, I would always take him out a cup of tea and a couple of chocolate biscuits. He loved his chocolate biscuits.'

'Mr Patel sells them,' I said but stopped myself, realising that I was interrupting one of Mrs Dawson's 'stories'. Mrs Dawson's stories could go on for at least half an hour and most related to some important event that had happened during her lifetime.

'And that's how I found him,' continued Mrs Dawson, 'one Saturday morning at 11am, sat in his favourite deckchair, as dead as a doornail.'

'That's sad,' I said, uncertain as to what the right words were to say when someone tells you of their husband's death.

'Oh, well, it's how he would have liked to have gone,' she said. 'I do miss him though.'
I avoided eye contact with Mrs Dawson, worried that she might be shedding a tear and might not want me to see. She reached into her handbag and pulled out a small cotton handkerchief which was embroidered with her initials, in green, in the corner. She gently dabbed her eyes before returning the hanky back into her bag. We sat quietly for several minutes staring out across the pond following the path of the randy duck. I said nothing because I was worried that anything I did say might be the wrong thing.

'This bench isn't particularly comfortable,' said Mrs Dawson, breaking the silence, as she wiggled from side to side. 'It will be some cheap Chinese rubbish. They don't make them like they used to.'
I looked down at the bench, it looked pretty much the same as all the others in the park to me.

'Will I see you in the library tomorrow?' I asked.

'Oh yes,' replied Mrs Dawson. 'I quite fancy reading Rebecca by Daphne Du Maurier again.'
Mrs Dawson loved Daphne Du Maurier. 'Her books draw you in,' she'd once said. She'd read every novel by Daphne Du Maurier several times but still kept taking them out.

'You should buy your own copies,' I said. 'Then you could read them whenever you wanted.'

'It's not the same,' replied Mrs Dawson. 'And anyway, I like my visits to the library and I like seeing you.'
She looked skywards towards the heavens.

'It never did rain,' she said.

Chapter Three

      The alarm clock went off at 5.30am. It was one of those large bedside clocks with brass bells on the top. My mother had bought it for me when I'd first moved to London several years previously. I was awake long before it decided it was time to get me up. It was still dark outside but a lone blackbird had been singing for at least half an hour. I got up slowly and caught my reflection in the wardrobe mirror, bleary-eyed and hair standing on end. I turned sideways, had I put on weight?

      I had a quick shower, got dressed and sat down and had a bowl of cornflakes at the kitchen table by the window. Mr Patel had them on special offer. They weren't Kelloggs but were close enough, as close as you could get for 78p. I gazed out on to the street. The street lamps were still on, their low powered lighting not disturbing the many people still in bed. This time of the day was glorious. There were no people and few cars. Even the birds were still asleep. Well, most of them anyway; the blackbird was singing its heart out.

From my window, I could look down the street to Mr Patel's. The lights of his shop were already on. I wondered if he ever closed. Perhaps the family took it in turns to work shifts to keep the shop open 24 hours a day. I could just make out Mr Patel outside his shop surveying his kingdom before the sun came up and his working day started all over again.

I glanced over to Norman's, his curtains were already open. For a few seconds, I stared at the empty window before he appeared, sat down with a cup of tea and produced a biscuit. I looked away before he saw me. I didn't want him to think that I was spying on him.

Fridays were funny days. Every Friday felt like no other day of the week. It was like it was the end of something, like everything was winding down. The weekend for most, spelled two days off work before the whole process started again on Monday. I liked Fridays. In fact, I loved Fridays. Even if I did work the following day in the charity shop. Although I saw that more as a hobby than a job.

Mr Peters had wanted us in the library at 7am, a whole two hours before we opened to the general public. He wanted to discuss something with us, something that couldn't wait until Monday morning, it seemed. I didn't mind the early start. It gave me the chance to return the Joanna Cannon book I'd borrowed without scanning it out. The Trouble With Goats and Sheep told the story of two little girls in 1976. Was 1976 really like that? I was too young to know. I'd have to ask Mrs Dawson who had a tale for every year of her life.

I left the house at 6.30am, carefully shutting

the front door quietly behind me, worried that I might awaken some sleeping neighbour. It was getting much lighter. Many of the other birds had taken the blackbird's cue and were now singing as loudly as they possibly could. I loved the sound of birdsong. It was a short walk to work, along the leafy streets to the 1960s pre-fab-type building that now served as the area's public library.

Mr Peters was waiting at the entrance when I arrived.

'It's a lovely day,' he said. 'The air is so fresh.' He breathed in deeply and exhaled with a loud 'ahh!'

'Yes,' I replied. 'I love early mornings, it's so peaceful.'

Mr Peters' moustache had been perfectly groomed and knitted into cat tails, ready for another day's work. He always wore a tweed jacket and a bow tie, either red or bright yellow. He was unlike anyone else who worked in the library.

'He's an odd character,' Mrs Dawson had once said but to me, he wasn't odd at all. He was just, well, different. But then weren't we all?
Mr Peters smiled.

'We're all gathering in the main room,' he said. 'I've an announcement to make.'
He smiled, said no more and I made my way past him into the library. Mrs Finnegan had pinned a leaflet to the notice board advertising a coffee morning the following Wednesday for people who were feeling lonely and 'wanted to make new friends'. I decided that I would photocopy it later and give a copy to Mrs Dawson.
I'd arrived early but most of the staff were already there. Miss Taylor, dressed entirely in black, as she

always was, shuffled some papers and generally tidied up before the meeting got under way. She didn't say much. Mrs Dawson had once said, 'That one's too wrapped up in her own self-importance.' She only ever smiled when Mr Peters was around and then her personality suddenly changed, not being able to do enough for people. She looked up at me over her half-moon glasses but neither looked pleased or displeased to see me.

'Good morning,' I said. 'It's lovely out.'
Miss Taylor just said a quiet 'yes' in response but no more. She was a woman in her fifties, still dressing as she had, no doubt, in her twenties. I don't think that there was a Mr Taylor or, if there was, he was never mentioned.

'That woman looks like a witch,' Mrs Dawson had once said rather unfairly although I agreed with her entirely.
Brian Carson and young, spotty Callum Rogers were also there as was Cecilia Moorhouse who was in charge of the reference section. She was very popular with people researching their family trees and with local historians, strange people with Co-op carrier bags, cardigans and zip-up anoraks. The anoraks loved local history as did Cecilia. I don't think that she liked me very much. Local history had its place but I wanted to read something more modern, something upbeat. I was currently reading The Lido by Libby Page which made me feel like I should really get into swimming again. Perhaps Mrs Dawson would come with me. I didn't know if she liked swimming or not, she certainly hadn't mentioned it.
Brian Carson liked high-class literature. He was the only person I knew who had read all of Tolstoy's War

and Peace. It didn't appeal to me. Callum Rogers read a lot of science fiction-type books, The War of the Worlds, The Day of the Triffids and such like. I'd seen him go into The Final Frontier shop with its window display of strange characters from Star Wars, a film, I'm embarrassed to say, I'd never seen. I preferred the old black and white Sunday afternoon classics such as Some Like It Hot or Gone With the Wind. Anything with James Stewart was a delight.

Callum bought endless comics, or 'the funny papers' as Mrs Dawson called them, from The Final Frontier. He kept them neatly packed in polythene covers stored in boxes in his bedroom. He'd invited me around to see them but I'd never gone.

Mr Peters coughed loudly.

'Can I have your attention please,' he said. 'Can you all gather around?'

There was something ominous in his tone.

'I received a letter from the council earlier this week,' he said, 'and I'm afraid to say that they plan to close our library down on 22nd June.'

His voice went slightly shaky when he said the word 'close' and for a second, I thought that he might cry. He held it together though.

'Surely not,' said Brian Carson. 'This library has been here longer than most of the people who work here can remember.'

'It's disgraceful,' said Miss Taylor. 'What are we to do? What about our jobs?'

I stayed quiet, carefully watching Mr Peters doing his best to keep calm while the world around him fell apart.

'We're to be merged with the Central Library,' said Mr Peters. 'I'm afraid I don't know what's going to happen to your jobs.'

'But that's three miles away,' said Brian. 'What about our regulars, the elderly, the ones who come here for the company, for a chat? They're not going to want to travel three miles to take a book out.'

'What about my coffee mornings?' Mrs Finnegan piped up.

Mr Peters shrugged his shoulders. Even his well-groomed moustache seemed to lose some of its shine.

'That's all I know, I'm afraid,' he said. 'It's all to do with council budgets and cuts.'

'Well, it won't do,' said Miss Taylor, looking even more angry than she normally did.

'I'm not sure there's much we can do,' said Mr Peters.

He thanked us and returned to his office looking forlorn. After a while, everyone returned to their various posts around the library.

'I could always get a job with the local butcher,' announced Callum. 'He's looking for an apprentice.'

'I thought that you were a vegetarian,' I said. Callum didn't answer and headed off to the children's section to re-shelve some recently returned books.

The library was unusually quiet all morning. It was as if even the building was slightly depressed. Mrs Dawson came in at about 2pm. She placed a copy of Rebecca down in front of me.

'Hello, dear,' she said. 'It's very quiet in here today, isn't it? Has someone died?'

'They want to close us down,' I said as I scanned her card and stamped her book.

'But they can't do that,' said Mrs Dawson. 'Where would I get my books?'

'They're going to merge us with the Central

Library,' I said. 'I'll have to find another job.'

Mrs Dawson looked concerned.

'We'll have a campaign, a protest,' she said, 'to keep the library open.'

'I'm not sure it will work,' I replied. 'It sounds like it's all done and dusted.'

'You can't give up,' said Mrs Dawson. She tapped the back of my hand slightly as if to re-assure me in some way.

'Oh, there's a coffee morning next Wednesday,' I said handing Mrs Dawson a leaflet I'd photocopied earlier.

'Will you still be open next week?' she asked.

'We're not closing until June,' I replied.

'Then we'll have a meeting, here,' said Mrs Dawson. 'Next Wednesday. Can you get some leaflets printed up?'

'I'll ask Mrs Ferguson,' I said, 'but I doubt it will do any good.'

'I'll get on to the newspapers, the tv, the radio,' continued Mrs Dawson. 'We'll have some sort of protest.'

'I'll have to discuss it with Mr Peters,' I said. We both looked over to Mr Peters who was searching for a book for a customer in the oversized books section.

'Alf loved a protest,' said Mrs Dawson. 'We protested when they shut the old Odeon down.'

'Did it do any good?' I asked.

'Not really,' she replied. 'They were showing The Bounty, the one with Mel Gibson. I didn't care for it much but Alf liked the scenery. He said we'd go to Tahiti one day, not that we ever did of course.'

'Oh,' I said, half-listening.
I could see Mr Peters talking to someone in the corner. But surely it was Norman Drudge, our reclusive neighbour.

'Don't look now,' I said to Mrs Dawson, 'but isn't that Norman over there?'
Mrs Dawson took no notice about 'not looking now' and turned quickly to look.

'Why, yes,' she said. 'There he is with that funny man with the moustache.'

'That's Mr Peters,' I said.

'Of course,' said Mrs Dawson. 'That reminds me, I must get a pint of milk on the way home.'

'How does it remind you?' I asked.

'The man in the shop has a moustache,' she replied. 'Of course, it's not so comical as Mr Peters'.'
I hadn't thought of Mr Peters' moustache being comical before, just different. It did get a lot of comments from the customers though.

'I wonder what they're talking about?' asked Mrs Dawson. 'Shall I go and listen?'

'You don't want to appear too obvious,' I replied.

'Mr Peters doesn't look at all happy,' said Mrs Dawson. 'He's got the sort of face my Alf used to give me whenever I cooked him spaghetti. He hated spaghetti. It was far too continental for our tastes.'

'I like spaghetti,' I said.

'I don't mind it out of a tin, dear,' she said, 'but I can't be bothering with the other stuff.'

'Look,' I said. 'Mr Peters is waving his arms around. He doesn't look at all happy.'
Norman did his best to calm him down but Mr Peters looked upset, slightly red-faced.

31

'I don't think I've ever seen him looking so flustered,' said Mrs Dawson.

Their conversation finished and Norman left the building.

'Quick,' I said. 'He's coming, pretend we haven't noticed anything.'

Mrs Dawson looked down at her book before picking it up and nonchalantly flicking through its pages.

'Yes, I particularly like Daphne Du Maurier,' she said, as if to appear that we were in deep conversation about the author.

'She's such a good writer, isn't she?' I said.

Mrs Dawson nodded as Mr Peters checked some books which had been returned and were lying on the counter beside me.

'Is everything alright?' I asked.

'That was Gerald Williams,' he said, 'the man from the council, the one who's closing us down.'

'Gerald?' Mrs Dawson exclaimed. 'He doesn't look much like a Gerald to me. Norman is a far better name.'

She took her book and turned to leave.

'I'll see you later, dear,' she said.

We both watched Mrs Dawson leave through the automatic doors, although they didn't seem particularly automatic today.

'We'll have to get them fixed,' said Mr Peters as he sorted through the books. 'Er, who's Norman?'

Chapter Four

Mrs Walters had taken receipt of a rather large quantity of vinyl long playing records when I arrived at the charity shop on Saturday morning.

'They were at the door when I opened up,' she said. 'Piles of them.'

'I've heard they're suddenly very collectable,' I said as she flicked through the collection.

'Des O'Connor, Max Bygraves, The Nolans,' said Mrs Walters. 'Oh, and The Black and White Minstrels.'

'Put that to one side,' I said. 'Mrs Dawson would like that.'

'I doubt that even Mrs Dawson would have a record player nowadays,' said Mrs Walters. 'And anyway, isn't it a bit well, er, racist?'

I looked up and down the cover and turned it over.

'I don't think anyone will be bothered,' I said, looking at a collection of men on the front cover with

blacked-up faces, holding canes and straw boaters.
I could see that Mrs Walters wasn't so sure.

'Mr Thompson, him with the toy shop,' said
Mrs Walters. 'He had a golliwog in the window and the
police were called. People don't like this sort of thing
anymore.'
I looked down at the cover again. I supposed that
people might find it offensive although I could see
nothing wrong with it myself.

'I'll put it out the back until Mrs Dawson
comes,' Mrs Walters said. 'We'll keep it out of view of
the general public.'

'Perhaps we should put some police tape
around it,' I said sarcastically.
Mrs Walters didn't answer, she was too engrossed
looking through the records which obviously brought
back many happy memories.

'Ah, Frank Sinatra,' she said. 'I had my first
dance to Strangers in the Night. That's what me and Mr
Walters were - Strangers in the Night.'
The bell over the door rang as our first customer
entered. It was Mrs Dawson.

'Hello, dear,' she said. 'How are you bearing
up?'
Mrs Walters gave me a sideways glance.

'Is something wrong?' she asked.

'Young Gemma is losing her job at the library,'
said Mrs Dawson. 'It's closing down.'

'Oh, I am sorry,' said Mrs Walters. 'What will
you do?'

'I don't know,' I replied. 'I'm sure something
will turn up.'

'Even so,' continued Mrs Walters. 'It's a great
worry for you.'

34

Mrs Dawson placed her handbag down on the counter.

'We're having a protest,' she announced. 'I had some leaflets run off at the printers down in the precinct. I spent all yesterday putting them through people's letter boxes and handing them out in the street.'

'I could have printed them up at work,' I said.

'It's alright, dear,' said Mrs Dawson. 'They were very cheap and time is of the essence.'

Mrs Dawson took one of the leaflets out of her handbag. It was one of those leather-types with a gold clasp on the top. She may have even bought it in the charity shop. I didn't like to ask.

'There's a meeting next week at the library,' she said to Mrs Walters. 'Everyone's welcome and the library's laying on coffee and biscuits.'

'Count me in,' said Mrs Walters taking the leaflet. 'I'll pin this up on the noticeboard.'

She left to find some drawing pins.

'Oh, I've something for you in the back room,' I said.

'That sounds ominous,' said Mrs Dawson, wondering what I could have concealed in the back room. I fetched the record and handed it to her.

'It came in this morning,' I said.

'Oh,' she said, scrutinising the cover. 'I thought that you'd found one of those Siamese cats looking into a wine glass.'

She looked disappointed but then smiled.

'This is lovely too,' she said. 'Alf did like George Chisholm.'

'We all stared at the cover.

'Which one is he?' I asked.

'The one on the left,' Mrs Dawson replied, as if

it was obvious.

Mrs Walters, by now, had returned with her drawing pins and looked closely at the cover.

'They all look the same to me,' she said.

Mrs Walters left us alone to continue sorting through the records.

'I meant to ask you earlier,' I said.

'What's that, dear?' Mrs Dawson asked.

'What was 1976 like?' I asked.

Mrs Dawson thought about it for a second or two.

'It was hot,' she replied. 'Alf wore shorts for most of the summer. Why do you ask?'

'Just a book I was reading,' I said.

'It was the hottest summer I can remember,' said Mrs Dawson. 'We had standpipes at the end of the street. Alf hated that, carrying a bucket of water back and forwards.'

'Oh,' I said.

'I remember him dragging tarmac in, the road had melted with the heat,' continued Mrs Dawson. 'We'd only had that carpet a week. It was a lovely yellow colour. Well, it was until Alf walked all over it.

'Oh,' I said again.

'We never did get it off,' said Mrs Dawson. 'We had to put an occasional table over the offending area.'

Mrs Dawson gazed down at the record again.

'I don't suppose you've got a record player,' I said.

'Oh yes I have,' she replied. 'I shall play this tonight. Leslie Crowther was one for a while. Do you remember him?'

I had to admit that I didn't. I didn't know most of the old stars that Mrs Dawson mentioned.

'The Price Is Right,' said Mrs Dawson. 'Come

on down', he used to say.'
She looked at me as if a mention of his catchphrase
would jog my memory. It didn't.

'He was on Crackerjack also,' she said.
It meant nothing.

'I'm going to put a pound on these LPs,' Mrs
Walters shouted across.
Mrs Dawson reached into her purse.

'It's alright,' I said. 'This one's free. It's on me.'

'That very kind of you, dear,' said Mrs Dawson
looking pleased as if I'd given her the crown jewels.
She wandered over to the knick-knack section and
looked up and down the shelves. She picked up a snow
globe which contained a view of New York, gave it a
shake and placed it back on the shelf.

'We've got four days to organise everything,'
she said. 'Try and get as many people at the meeting as
possible. I've contacted Councillor Evans. I know he's
an arse but he always seems to be able to attract plenty
of attention.'
I hadn't heard Mrs Dawson say 'arse' before, or any
other swear word but in desperate situations, perhaps it
was needed. Anyway Councillor Evans was an arse, all
16 stone of him.

Chapter Five

I got up late on Sunday morning, well 9.30 am which was late for me. I pulled the blind up in the kitchen and there was Norman, looking through his binoculars towards number 10. I stared across at him for a while before he put his binoculars down beside him and picked up a mug of tea. I didn't want him to see me so I pulled backwards. I shook the box of cornflakes on the side, they were almost empty. I would have to take a trip down to Mr Patel's later in the day to get another. Patel's opened all Sunday, in fact it opened every day, even Christmas.

I sat at the table with my bowl of cornflakes staring out towards the street. Mr Bishop across the way was fiddling with his car as usual. It was very old, I think he said that it was a Ford Anglia. It was bright yellow, the colour of a lemon, and had fins where the lights at the back were. It was certainly different from all the other cars in the street. When Mr Bishop wasn't adjusting something under the bonnet, he'd spend his time washing and polishing his 'pride and joy', as Mrs Bishop called it.

'He could have bought a brand new one,' she'd once said to me, 'with all the money he's spent on that thing.'

Mr Bishop was well into his sixties and I assumed he'd had the car from new. He'd retired several years before, he'd been some sort of aeronautics engineer, working in a factory, somewhere across the other side of the city. He dressed in baggy corduroy trousers kept up by a pair of white braces. He always wore a short sleeved shirt, together with a patterned tank top. Mrs Dawson said that he looked like he'd come from another age. The Bishops fostered two young children, David and Susie, although they weren't seen playing out very often. On Sundays, the whole Bishop family took the Ford Anglia 'for a spin', to visit relatives or the countryside and, presumably, to see if the car was still working.

I'd planned a lazy day in although the sun was shining and I really felt that I should be out and about doing something. There was a good Cary Grant film on at 2pm but I decided that watching the television in the afternoon was a rainy, cold winter day sort of thing to do. No, I decided to get dressed, go to Patel's and get another 59p loaf and go to the park and feed the ducks. I needed cornflakes but I would get them on the way back, I didn't want to carry them around the park all day. Two visits to Patel's would break up the day a bit, I reasoned.

'Hello, Miss Davies,' said Mr Patel as I entered his shop. The brass bell above the door continued to ring even after I'd entered. It was the oldest part of the shop, even older than Mr Patel Senior.

'It's Gemma,' I said. 'Please call me Gemma.'
Mr Patel smiled. He held out his hand to shake mine. It seemed an odd thing to do but I shook my shopkeeper's hand.

'Hello, Gemma,' he said. 'My name is Paul.'
I hadn't expected him to be called Paul for some reason. I expected him to have a more exotic name such as Deepak or Vikram. We already had too many 'Pauls' in the area. The man who walked his two Westies past my door every morning was called Paul, as was the electrician who lived down the road. The postman was called Paul, there was a Paul at the library as well as a Paul who drove the number 29 bus. Even the poor homeless man who slept in a tent in the park, and tended to drink too much, was called Paul. Mrs Dawson regularly bought 'Homeless Paul' something to eat as well as giving him several of Mr Dawson's old clothes. She'd knitted him a nice woolly jumper in the winter although he'd said that he didn't particularly care for red and complained that the sleeves were too long.

'Are you going to the park?' asked Indian Paul. 'We've a special offer on bread, only 49p a loaf.'
Mr Patel had made a display out of several loafs of bread, piling them on top of each other, with a cardboard 'star' with the word 'reduced' written on it. A line had been drawn through '59p' and 'now only 49p' was written underneath.

'Is this fresh?' I asked.

'It's only two days out of date,' said Mr Patel. 'I'm sure the ducks won't mind.'
I realised as I searched through my purse for 49p that I knew very little about Mr Patel. I'd been coming in his shop for several years but apart from his name, I knew

nothing about him.

'It's a lovely day,' I said. 'Will you be going out later today?'

'I've got the shop to run,' he said. '24/7.'

I smiled. There seemed to be something different about Mr Patel today. As Mr Patel, he seemed to just be our local shopkeeper but as 'Paul', he seemed far more personable.

'I get Thursday afternoons off,' he said. 'My father runs the shop then.'

'Oh, I go to the park on Thursday afternoons,' I said. 'With Mrs Dawson.'

'Ah, yes, Mrs Dawson,' said Mr Patel. 'Her husband liked Shreddies.'

'He did,' I laughed.

'I might see you in the park on Thursday,' said Mr Patel. 'And Mrs Dawson, of course.'

I left the shop smiling. Had Mr Patel, Paul, just arranged a date with me? No, of course not, I reasoned, he was just being friendly.

I arrived at the park and sat on our favourite bench. It was the one with the brass plaque which read, 'For Iris, she loved this place'. I had no idea who Iris had been but I imagined her exactly where I was, sitting feeding the ducks.

I saw Mrs Dawson talking to a couple of men in the distance. This was unusual for a Sunday. Mrs Dawson usually visited her sister, Alice, on a Sunday. I'd never met Alice but she had a Persian cat and a husband called Eric. Mrs Dawson always had her Sunday dinner at Alice's.

She walked over when she saw me.

'Hello, dear,' she said.

'What are you doing here?' I asked.

'Alice had to go to the hospital,' she replied.

'Is she okay?' I asked.

'Oh, yes,' she replied. 'Eric managed to drill a hole in his hand. It went clear through. He's hopeless with power tools.'

'Is he going to be alright?' I inquired.

'There was blood everywhere,' replied Mrs Dawson. 'Mr Culshaw next door took them both up to the A&E department. They had to wait four hours. She never did get her shelf put up.'

Mrs Dawson sat down and we both looked out across the pond. There were no ducks today, they must have found a better eatery.

'Who were you talking to?' I asked.

'When?' replied Mrs Dawson.

'Just then,' I said. 'To those two men.'

'Oh, them,' replied Mrs Dawson. 'I was telling them about the library closure. I've been telling everyone and handing out leaflets.'

'Were they interested?' I asked.

'Not particularly,' she replied, 'That's what people are like nowadays but they might mention it to someone else who is interested, I suppose.'

Mrs Dawson smiled as we both watched a small, bald headed man running erratically on the spot.

'He'll do himself an injury doing that,' she said. 'Why can't people just take things easy? Oh, he's stretching now. What does he look like?'

We watched as the man reached into the air with both arms before bending in half before straightening up and standing on one leg, desperately trying to pull his other leg behind his back.

'Oh,' said Mrs Dawson. 'That won't do him any good. It looks very painful, doesn't it, dear?'

'Yes,' I replied, staring towards the pond to see if any ducks had appeared.

A seagull swooped in, squawking for attention.

'I did enjoy that record,' said Mrs Dawson. 'The one featuring The Black and White Minstrels. It brought back so many memories.'

'I'm pleased,' I replied. 'There are many more in the shop. We haven't managed to sell any. Everyone has i-pods nowadays and download their music from the internet.'

'Oh, I couldn't be doing with that,' said Mrs Dawson.

'It's easy,' I said. 'Even Mr Peters at the library has one.'

There was a couple of seconds silence before the seagull began squawking again.

'Oh, no, dear, I don't think I could be bothered with any of that,' said Mrs Dawson. 'I'm afraid technology has passed me by, I won't catch up now.'

'But it's easy,' I repeated. 'I could show you.'

'No, it's okay, dear,' said Mrs Dawson. 'And anyway, I want something you can hold, something you can feel. There's nothing quite like a long playing record, its cover, the smell of the vinyl, the clicks and clacks as it plays. You get none of that from a download.'

'No,' I said. 'But it's convenient. You can fit thousands of tunes on an i-pod.'

'I know, dear,' said Mrs Dawson, 'but it's not for me. Alice wanted to buy me a Kindle last Christmas. A Kindle, I ask you?'

I knew what Mrs Dawson meant. I'd avoided buying a Kindle myself. I loved the feel, the look and the smell of a good book. A machine could never offer you that, could it?

A lone duck landed and started to quack loudly. I produced the loaf of bread and handed it to Mrs Dawson who unwrapped it and started to break pieces off.

'I think that I might have a date,' I said.

'A date?' replied Mrs Dawson. 'Who with?

'Mr Patel from the shop,' I replied. 'Next Thursday.'

'A date with the shopkeeper?' said Mrs Dawson. 'With Mr Patel, him with the cheap bread and the dodgy Shreddies?'

'Yes,' I replied. 'Only it might not be a date. He said that he has Thursday afternoon off and he might come for a walk in the park.'

'But Thursday's our day,' said Mrs Dawson.

'I told him that,' I replied. 'Anyway it probably isn't a date. I suppose he's just going for a walk.'
Mrs Dawson broke up more bread and scattered it around our feet.

'My first date with Alf was at the Odeon,' said Mrs Dawson. 'We saw The Guns of Navarone with Gregory Peck. It wasn't very romantic.'

'I don't think I've seen it,' I said.

'It was all shooting and fighting and David Niven,' said Mrs Dawson. 'Alf bought me a bunch of flowers. What was I supposed to do with a bunch of flowers for two hours?'
I threw a piece of bread to the lone duck who was shortly joined by another and then another.

'Don't let the shopkeeper take you to see The Guns of Navarone,' said Mrs Dawson.
Calling Paul 'the shopkeeper' already suggested to me that Mrs Dawson didn't approve of the idea.

44

'It's probably not a date,' I said. 'Just two people in the same place at the same time.'

'You could tell him about the library,' said Mrs Dawson. 'The more people who know, the better.'

'He won't be interested in the library,' I said.

'He reads, doesn't he?' said Mrs Dawson.

'I hardly know him,' I replied, realising that I was being silly to suggest that two people bumping into each other in a park was a date.

'Norman was watching the woman with the big chest again,' I said, as Mrs Dawson threw a piece of bread which bounced off the randy duck's head.

'It's very odd,' said Mrs Dawson. 'Maybe he's some sort of Peeping Tom. There used to be a man where we used to live, always looking through people's windows. Mrs Blackburn's underwear went missing.'

'How odd,' I said.

'Yes,' replied Mrs Dawson. 'It was there in the evening on the washing line and gone the next morning. Heaven knows what he did with it.'

'Did the police catch him?' I asked.

'Oh, yes,' replied Mrs Dawson. 'It was all in the papers. Reginald Simms, I think his name was.'

'How embarrassing,' I said.

'It's nothing compared to what they get up to nowadays,' said Mrs Dawson but said no more.

'He just sits there everyday with his binoculars,' I continued. 'Always watching, always keeping an eye on number 10.'

'Maybe he's doing something else,' suggested Mrs Dawson.'Maybe it's something to do with his job. Maybe he doesn't just shut down libraries. He works for the council, he could be up to anything.'

We pondered what he could be up to as the randy duck

chased the other ducks around the pond.

'Maybe he's checking to see if people are putting the right stuff in their recycling bins,' said Mrs Dawson.

'Maybe,' I said.

'Or perhaps he's checking to see whose dogs are fouling in the street,' said Mrs Dawson. 'I ruined a perfectly good pair of shoes there last Tuesday.'

'That's awful,' I said.

'I know whose dog it is,' said Mrs Dawson. 'It's the border collie that belongs to that man with the rather large stomach who prances around in tight denim shorts all day.'

'The one who's always cleaning his caravan?' I asked.

'Yes,' Mrs Dawson replied. 'I don't know what he thinks he looks like. He lets that dog do its business wherever it wants.'

I smiled.

'I suppose Mr Patel was just being polite,' I said. 'He probably hasn't got any plans to walk in the park on Thursday.'

Chapter Six

I was up early at 5.30am on Monday morning. Usually, I had a lie-in until 7am before I got ready and made my way to work. I'd been unable to sleep for most of Sunday night. I don't know if it was because it was unusually stuffy or the thought of the library closure and my impending unemployment was playing on my mind. Even thinking about meeting Mr Patel in the park circulated around my head. After trying to sleep in every position, I finally decided to get up and stay up. I didn't like to pull the curtains that early in the morning, you never knew who might be looking in. I peeped out of a gap at the side and looked out towards the street. It was eerily quiet. A lone blackbird sang somewhere off into the distance. I looked up into the sky and could see the half moon reflecting its light on the houses below. A sly glance took my eyes across to Norman's house, expecting him to be sat there, drinking tea and eating biscuits. The window was empty. I suppose even Norman had to sleep sometime.

I boiled the kettle and made myself some coffee. Mr Patel had been selling off sachets of cappuccino, twelve in a box for 89p. The packaging was strangely in Arabic for some reason. I hoped that the contents were actually coffee, I hadn't asked, but there was a picture of a cup with someone pouring water into it, so I assumed that it was.

I stirred the contents into a mug, a 'builder's mug' as Mrs Dawson would say, poured on water and gave it a stir. I sniffed it carefully. It certainly smelled like coffee, it looked like coffee and I gingerly took a sip. It had an unusual taste but wasn't altogether unpleasant so I sat at the kitchen table drinking it slowly.

I reached over for the remote control and turned on the television. The BBC News was on - all doom and gloom and Dan Walker. I watched it for a while, half awake, wondering if the forthcoming library closure would be mentioned on the local news. I turned the sound down while I waited for the regional news. Kim Jong-un's face appeared.

'Maybe if he ever makes friends with Donald Trump,' Mrs Dawson had said, 'they'll get him a proper suit and a nice hair cut. He could do with losing some weight as well.'

The story, whatever it was, was going on and on, so I turned the television off, got washed and dressed and drew the curtains and pulled up the blind. As I reached for my cornflakes, there was Norman, smartly dressed in suit and tie, drinking tea and dunking, what appeared to be, a Hob-Nob.

I'd totally forgotten about my alarm clock which went off at 7am with a loud ring. I rushed to the bedroom to turn it off, tripping over my slippers. They were the ones with the fluffy insoles that Mrs Dawson had bought me two Christmases previously.

'You'll get chilblains in this cold flat if you're not careful,' she'd said at the time.

I returned to the kitchen and looked across the street but Norman had already gone, probably on his way to work to finalise his plan for closing us down. I picked up my keys and the copy of The Lido which I had to return to the library. There had been several requests for it during the week but all our copies were out on loan. I preceded along Winslow Place, it's old slate paving stones gleaming with the morning dew. Mr Graves said 'Good morning' to me, as he did most days. He'd been a policeman at one time but had long since retired. He seemed to find difficulty knowing what to do with his time and spent most of it sweeping around the front of his house or trimming his hedges. His wife had once worked on a fruit stall but nowadays spent most of her time indoors, watching the television. I'd passed her many times on my way to work but she would never speak. I think she thought that I wasn't good enough for her.

'She's just jealous because you're young and pretty,' Mrs Dawson had said before calling her 'a miserable old trout.'

On I walked down the tree lined lanes of Rennie Avenue, along Marsh Road with its dilapidated terraced houses, up Cornwall Street towards Portland Road where the library was based near to the communal tennis courts and playing fields. The whole journey took me about ten minutes if I walked quickly, fifteen if I strolled.

Mr Peters was busy arranging the shelves when I arrived.

'We've got to have the place looking tidy,' he said. 'There's an inspection today.'

'What inspection?' I asked. 'Nobody told me.'

'Councillor Evans and some of his cronies are paying us a visit,' said Mr Peters. 'It was all very last minute.'

It seemed odd that there was an inspection if we were due to be closed down any day.

'It's not an inspection,' said Miss Taylor abruptly. 'It's just Councillor Evans showing his face, trying to glean publicity. No doubt he'll have a press photographer with him.'

'They're just going through the paces,' said Mr Peters. 'You know Councillor Evans. He likes to appear that he's doing his best for everyone and then does nothing.'

It was true. He'd promised to tidy up the nearby tennis courts and playing fields but they'd remained unusable for at least two years. They were surrounded by high mesh fence with a sign saying 'Danger : Do Not Enter'. A hole had been cut in the fence by inquisitive children who raced their BMX bikes around the dilapidated fields, ignoring any of the 'Danger' signs which were covered in graffiti.

I got my copy of The Lido out of my shopping bag, scanned it and placed it back on the shelf. I looked at it for a few seconds knowing that it would soon be taken out again. Someone else would soon have all the joy and wonder that I'd had over the previous few days reading it. I needed something new and uplifting. Most of our latest fiction books seemed to be crime novels which weren't for me at all. I decided to read Three Things About Elsie by Joanna Cannon. It had a nice colourful cover showing a Battenberg cake. The cover alone made me hungry. I decided to get some sort of cake on the way home from Mr Patel's. I could share it with Mrs Dawson on Thursday, I thought. That is, if I hadn't eaten it all by then.

I returned to the front desk, scanned the book and popped it into my bag. I decided that I would start it tonight when I got home.

I knew that someone was waiting so I hurried myself along before looking up. There in front of me stood Norman Drudge. I stared at him for a couple of seconds. I'd never seen him so close. He wasn't quite as old as I thought he was, 54 or 55 maybe. He pulled a small card out of his outside jacket pocket and handed it to me.

'Gerald Williams,' he said. 'I'm here to see Mr Peters.'

I looked at him intently. He obviously had no idea who I was. He had no idea that I lived just across the road from him, too busy staring at the lady at number 10's large chest.

'Mr Peters?' he repeated.

I already didn't like him. He seemed a very impatient sort of man to me. The cheek of him closing down our library. I bet that he'd never read a book in his life.

'I'll get him for you,' I replied before I set off to find Mr Peters who was hiding in the music section just to the left of Debussy.

'That man's here to see you,' I said, not wanting to say his name out loud. 'The one who wants to shut us down.'

'Oh,' said Mr Peters, poking his head around the shelf where a small bust of Beethoven stood.

'He never looks very happy,' I said.

'Mr Williams?' asked Mr Peters.

'No, I meant Beethoven,' I said. 'He always looks miserable in pictures or busts.'

'I suppose being deaf made him unhappy,' said Mr Peters. 'Did he say what he wanted, Mr Williams, that is.'

'No,' I replied. 'He just gave me his card. Do you think it's about the closure?'

'Probably,' said Mr Peters before tweaking his moustache and straightening his yellow bow tie. He put on his best fake smile and walked the ten feet to the front desk.

'Ah, Mr Williams,' he said, still smiling and holding his hand out to shake that of our visitor. 'What a pleasant surprise.'

They shook hands. It wasn't a warm hand shake, it was far more superficial than that. I imagined that Norman had very sweaty, clammy hands anyway and that Mr Peters wouldn't want to grab one too tight.

I watched the pair as I arranged Bach, Beethoven and Berlioz in the right order. Who had put Berlioz before Beethoven, I wondered?

I watched Mr Peters lead Norman to one of the reading tables. He would always be Norman to me, I couldn't bring myself to ever think of him as a Gerald. I looked at the card he'd given to me, all gold embossed and letters after his name, one final time before depositing it in the metal bin placed at the end of the shelf next to Gaetano Donizetti. I loved the music section.

Norman had a strange leather briefcase with a black plastic handle on top and brass pop-up catches, the sort that were popular with schoolboys in old movies from the 1970s. I saw him take out a few files and place some papers in front of Mr Peters. Surely he wasn't going to sign away our library. I thought about making them both a cup of coffee and then at the last second spilling it all over Norman and his papers but Miss Taylor had beaten me to it, haughtily placing two plastic beakers of coffee down on the table beside them. They got milk and sugar whether they wanted it or not. That's how Miss Taylor took it so that was how everyone else got it, even young spotty Callum Rogers who was diabetic.

Mr Peters and Norman talked for a while and drank their coffee. It all seemed quite amicable. Mr Peters picked up the papers, shuffled them together and stood up before shaking Norman's hand again once more. They both seemed quite happy. Maybe the library wasn't going to close after all.

As I watched, Miss Taylor came up suddenly behind me. She had a habit of doing this. I jumped.

'Those books won't put themselves on the shelves,' she said abruptly.

I wasn't about to let her intimidate me although she did her best.

'No, I don't suppose they will,' I replied.

Mrs Dawson particularly didn't like Miss Taylor.

'Just ignore her,' she said, which on the whole I did.

Mrs Dawson had called her, perhaps unfairly, 'a frustrated old lesbian.' Not in earshot, of course. Anyway, I did my best to keep out of Miss Taylor's way. She was polite, almost creepy, to Mr Peters but that was only because he was in charge. Callum Rogers used to spend long spells in the toilet just to avoid her but he had seemed to have got over his phobia of 'the old witch', as Brian Carson called her. Callum blamed Miss Taylor for his IBS and his doctor had put him on small green tablets which he had to take twice a day.

Apart from Norman's visit, the morning was pretty uneventful. Someone asked Mr Peters for a book called The Gentleman's Guide to Beard and Moustache Management and for about half an hour, they both seemed to be in their element.

'It's moments like that I'll miss,' said Mr Peters afterwards, 'when the library finally closes down.'

I had a walk to Patel's during my dinner break and picked up some Madeira cake. I looked around for Mr Patel but he was nowhere to be seen. Maybe I should have come in after work. I suddenly realised that I was actively seeking him out since he'd mentioned the walk in the park.

'Hello again,' said Mr Patel Senior, smiling, in his brown tank top. He lifted the Madeira cake up cautiously as if he'd never seen one before. Perhaps only English people ate Madeira cake, I thought. But, of course, that was ridiculous. Surely people in Madeira also ate it, didn't they?

'For the ducks?' he asked.

'It's for me,' I said, smiling, not sure if he was joking or not. 'For me and Mrs Dawson, that is.'

'Of course,' he said as he took the £1.50 from me and put it in the till.

'Is Paul not around today?' I asked quietly. He seemed surprised that I knew that he was called Paul. Most people just referred to him as Mr Patel, even Mr Patel Senior.

'He's at the wholesalers,' came the reply. 'Getting more Madeira cake.'
I think it was a joke. I smiled and picked up the cake and headed towards the door.

'He will be back this evening,' said Mr Patel Senior, as he waved a friendly goodbye.

As I walked briskly back to the library, Madeira cake in hand, I wondered why Mr Patel Senior had shared this information with me, 'he will be back this evening.' Had Mr Patel Junior been talking about me? Perhaps he liked me after all? I'd have to ask Mrs Dawson what she thought.

I arrived back at the library and carefully stored my Madeira cake in the fridge in the staff's eating area with a cardboard sign attached to it which read, 'Hands off!'

Councillor Evans arrived at 2pm sharp with two of his colleagues together with local reporter Dan Partridge and a photographer from The Chronicle. Partridge had aspirations to get a job with one of the leading newspapers but it wasn't going to happen. Covering the opening of fetes, charity bingo nights and, of course, the closure of local libraries was about his limit. He was a scruffy-looking sort of person, with tombstone teeth stained from smoking too many roll-up cigarettes. His clothes looked ill-fitting and unironed.

'That man could do with a good haircut,' Mrs Dawson had once said.

Mr Peters had had us tidy up the library in preparation of Councillor Evans's visit. We were all supposed to be polite and helpful towards him but it seemed that no-one had told Miss Taylor.

'Have you come to close us down?' she said abruptly as Councillor Evans entered the building. Councillor Evans looked taken aback.

'I've come to help,' he replied, looking slightly flustered. 'It's the opposition who want to close you down.'

He was referring to the Conservative run council and its leader, 'Jack' Smethurst. Smethurst's real first name was 'Ronald' but he got called Jack for some reason.

Many thought it was because it made him sound more personable but Mrs Dawson said that she thought that it came from an old 1970's sitcom called 'Love Thy Neighbour.'

'It starred him off Eastenders,' she said, but I was none the wiser.

Mr Peters smiled as he led Councillor Evans on a tour around the library. Dan Partridge took notes along the way.

'It's disgusting,' said Evans. 'The community needs their library. We intend to fight this proposed closure all the way.'

'Good luck with that,' said Miss Taylor sarcastically.

The Chronicle's photographer gathered us all together and took our photo for the following morning's paper. Callum wore his Support the Seal black t-shirt for the occasion. Miss Taylor refused to smile and folded her arms. Brian Carson held up a sign saying 'Save Our Library'. It was a very cosy sort of photo. Mr Peters looked impressive with his tartan waistcoat, bow tie and well-groomed moustache.

'There's a meeting, here in the library, on Wednesday,' I announced.

No-one was listening. They were all too busy following Councillor Evans around as he revealed his plans for the future of the library after it was saved.

The day was pretty uneventful after Councillor Evans and his entourage left. I returned to the staffroom to find that half of my Madeira cake had been eaten.

'I gave it to Councillor Evans,' said Miss Taylor, smiling for a change. 'He likes a bit of Madeira cake and I assured him that you wouldn't mind.'

She didn't wait for my reply but grabbed her coat and left. My cardboard 'hands off' notice lay in the grey metal bin beside the door.

'The cheek of the woman,' said Mrs Dawson as we sat in my kitchen that evening drinking tea and eating the rest of the cake.

'I suppose I could always have bought another,' I said.

'That's not the point,' replied Mrs Dawson. 'That woman should be taught a lesson.'

'Perhaps it will do some good,' I said. 'My Madeira cake and Councillor Evans on our side, maybe it will somehow keep the library open.'

'He's a greedy pig, I know that,' said Mrs Dawson.

We both stared out of the window towards Norman's house where he was sat drinking a cup of tea.

'He was in the library again earlier today,' I said. 'He gave me an embossed calling card.'

'Who?' asked Mrs Dawson.

'Norman,' I replied, nodding my head in his general direction. 'He'd come to see Mr Peters. They drank coffee and Norman gave him some papers. They looked quite happy.'

'I suppose Miss Taylor was milling around?' asked Mrs Dawson.

'Yes,' I replied. 'She made them some coffee. In plastic cups.'

'I'm surprised that she didn't give Norman your Madeira cake,' she said. 'Cheek of the woman.'

Mrs Dawson didn't usually come around in the evenings on Monday. She liked to settle in and watch Coronation Street although she always complained that it wasn't the same as it was in her day.

'What would Ena Sharples have said?' she would say often.

I wasn't sure who Ena Sharples was.

Mrs Dawson came to finalise the details for Wednesday's meeting at the library.

'I've pinned up notices everywhere I can think of,' she said. 'Mr Johnson's son works for the free local paper and said that they'll do a piece in there.'

Mr Johnson took Mrs Dawson out to the bingo on Friday nights and sometimes on day trips in his Austin Allegro. They weren't romantically linked, they were just good company for each other. Alf had been the only man for Mrs Dawson. Even so, they seemed to 'knock along' together very well.

Whenever I asked her if she would ever get married again, she'd always say, 'I don't want to be washing another man's underpants again'. It seemed a funny thing to say.

I put the kettle on to boil so that I could make another cup of tea. I'd bought a box of Mrs Dawson's favourite, PG Tips. Whenever we drank it, she always said that she missed the monkeys on the adverts.

'They used to get up to all sorts,' she laughed. 'Shifting pianos, plumbing, decorating, drinking tea.' The kettle made a noise as it boiled and steam blew through the whistle on its spout.

'Of course,' she continued. 'It's not politically correct to have a monkey drinking tea nowadays. I'm sure they enjoyed themselves. They always looked happy enough.'

I poured the water into the teapot and added two spoonfuls of tea. Mrs Dawson had given me a special spoon for the purpose that she'd bought in 1972 when she'd travelled to Scotland with Alf.

'A young man at the chemist held the door open for me this morning and called me madam,' said Mrs Dawson. 'It was most odd.'

'Oh?' I said.

'I suddenly felt very old,' said Mrs Dawson. 'He wouldn't have called a young lady madam, would he?'

'He might do,' I said. 'And, anyway, you're not old.'

'But I am, dear,' replied Mrs Dawson. 'Age has crept up on me without me noticing and now I'm an old woman.'

'You're only as old as you feel, isn't that what you're always telling me?' I said.

'What I'm saying, dear, is don't let life pass you by,' said Mrs Dawson. 'You're young one moment, out dancing, stepping out with a young man and the next you're an old woman whose only pleasure comes from sitting in front of the television watching Coronation Street reminiscing about a long-gone past life.'

'But you're not like that,' I said. 'And anyway, you've always got me.'

'I know, dear, and I'm very grateful for it,' said Mrs Dawson. 'I'm just saying don't let life pass you by. Don't get stuck in a rut. It's so easy to just let one day run into another.'

Mrs Dawson appeared to be particularly maudlin today and just because a young man had called her 'madam' in the chemist.

'But it's the little things that make your day, isn't it?' I said. 'Like our Thursday morning cups of tea, our walks around the park, finding your favourite movie is on the telly. You don't know what happy moments life holds for you around the corner.'

Mrs Dawson stared out of the window towards the

street.

'Of course, you're right, dear,' she said. 'I'm not sure why I'm being so miserable today. A young man can call a lady madam, can't he? I'm just being a daft old woman.'

I didn't know what to say to cheer Mrs Dawson up so just said what I usually said at times like these.

'Cup of tea?' I said, holding up the teapot.

Mrs Dawson smiled.

'That would be lovely, she said. 'Did you see Mr Patel today?'

'No,' I replied. 'He was out. Mr Patel Senior served me.'

'The one in the brown tank top?' Mrs Dawson inquired.

'Yes,' I replied. 'I was going to pop in again after work but after the fuss with the Madeira cake, I decided not to bother.'

Norman was on the move. We both watched him get out of his seat and disappear into his front room.

'I wonder if there's a Mrs Drudge?' asked Mrs Dawson.

'I've never seen one,' I replied.

'Oh well,' said Mrs Dawson. 'You know what civil servants are like.'

I carefully poured the tea into our two china cups making sure that I added a dash of milk first. Mrs Dawson watched me carefully.

'Is it recycling week, this week?' she asked.

'No, it's general waste,' I said, raising the cup to my lips and blowing on the tea gently.

'Only I'm never sure what's what,' continued Mrs Dawson. 'We had a leaflet through the door. Apparently, a plastic milk bottle goes into recycling, but its lid goes in general waste.'

'Oh,' I said, half listening, as I noticed Mr Patel walking towards his corner shop. He had a happy, sort of confident walk.

'I mean it's all plastic, isn't it?' Mrs Dawson continued. 'It's the same with Lucozade bottles. The bottle goes in recycling, the outer plastic and the top go in general waste. And you're not to put black plastic into recycling.'

I watched Mr Patel continue on his way, stopping only to say 'hello' to Mr Bishop as he cleaned his Ford Anglia.

'Did you get the leaflet, dear?' asked Mrs Dawson.

'I think it went in recycling,' I said.

'I suppose that's where it belongs,' replied Mrs Dawson.

'I bought the Madeira cake for us to eat on Thursday,' I said. 'But I can always get another.'

I produced Joanna Cannon's book Three Things About Elsie and showed it to Mrs Dawson.

'It's the cover,' I said. 'It made me feel like buying a fancy cake, I haven't had a Madeira cake for years.'

Mrs Dawson looked at the cover carefully, staring at the front before turning it over to look at the back. She placed it carefully down on the table.

'Councillor Evans must be reading it also,' she joked.

We drank our tea and watched as Norman reappeared with a mug of tea and a packet of what appeared to be Garibaldis.

'It gives you an excuse to pop in to see Mr Patel again,' said Mrs Dawson, smiling.

I suddenly realised that unconsciously I'd been searching for reasons to go into his shop.

'It's not like that,' I protested, realising that it probably was.

Chapter Seven

The noise of exploding fireworks kept me up until 2am. Not the usual pretty ones but the ones that didn't seem to do much but let out a tremendous bang. I'd gazed out at 12am but everybody's lights were off, even Norman's.

'How could they all sleep through this racket?' I thought.

It seemed odd letting fireworks off in May. There were many festivals and events celebrated in the area including Ramadan and Deepavali but I wasn't sure when they were or if they involved fireworks or not.

I settled down to read my book in the armchair in the front room. The tired, oversized seat had come with the flat, slightly worse for wear and covered in a strange, stripy material that was probably last fashionable in 1970. I should really have replaced it by now but it was comfy and it reminded me of all the cosy days I'd spent indoors reading, when it was either too cold to go out or I just fancied a quiet day at home. Anyway, it was so difficult getting anything delivered and I didn't fancy all the fuss of ordering a new one. I couldn't part with it anyway, it was like an old friend, like Mr Peters' cat, Malcolm. He wouldn't part with Malcolm and just get a new cat, would he?

My book reminded me to get more Madeira cake. I'd pop into Mr Patel's later on the way to work and get some more and make sure it was out of reach of Miss Taylor or Councillor Evans, if he popped into the library later and felt hungry.

I finally nodded off at about 3am. I think that the fireworks had stopped by then. Maybe my brain had just tuned them out. After a restless night, I found myself completely awake at 6.30am. The resident blackbird happily chirped outside my kitchen window. I gave him some crumbs on most days and he seemed quite happy with that. I got up out of the armchair. My book fell off my lap at page 126 but I'd jammed a bookmark, made out of cardboard from an old cornflakes packet, within its pages so that I didn't lose my place.

'You would think that a librarian would have a proper bookmark,' Mrs Dawson had once said while examining a pile of books I'd been reading. She had brought me back a lovely one that she'd bought on a trip to Cornwall but it seemed too nice to use. I kept in on the shelf with my read books that I planned to re-read again sometime in the future.

I went into the bathroom and looked in the mirror. I looked tired with black rings under my eyes. Perhaps I would give Mr Patel's a miss this morning. He wouldn't want to see me looking like this. But then again, he probably wasn't bothered. The other day was probably just friendly chit-chat. When I thought about it, he was like that to all his customers. No, I thought, I'd wake myself up with a shower, get dressed and go in Mr Patel's like I did on most days.

Winslow Place was unusually quiet for a Tuesday morning. No sign of our eternally-angry postman, no Mr Bishop cleaning his car, no Old Man Graves, as the kids liked to call him. I assumed that they had all been kept awake by the fireworks and were now taking the chance of a lie-in.

The bell rang on the door of Mr Patel's as I entered his shop. Mr Patel was busy packing the cereal shelf with packets of cornflakes, Weetabix, Shreddies and All-Bran.

'Mr Graves likes a box of All-Bran,' Mrs Graves had once said to Mr Patel when I was in the shop. 'It keeps him regular.'

I was happy to say a friendly 'hello' to Mr and Mrs Graves when I passed them but I didn't particularly want to know about Mr Graves' toilet habits. Although I did seem to get an update on people's operations and illness wherever I went. And these were from people I didn't know, or knew little, whilst I was standing at the bus stop or queueing in the post office. I was quite happy with the ones who just said, 'it looks like we're in for rain again' but I wasn't interested in the ins and outs of their hospital visits. Mrs Jacobson's husband Ronald had had his gallbladder out apparently but there was no explanation as to why. 'He's a completely different man,' she told me. Luckily, the 23 came along soon after, she was waiting for the 29. I'd have got on the 23 even if I didn't want the 23, just to get away from her.

Mr Patel stopped what he was doing and turned and smiled.

'Hello, Gemma,' he said. 'It's a beautiful day outside, isn't it?'

I was surprised that he called me Gemma or that he had even remembered my name but a slight smile came to my face, pleased that he had.

'Have you any Madeira cake?' I blurted out.

I wanted to have a proper, normal conversation with Mr Patel but it was the first thing that came to mind. He smiled.

'We seem to have had a run on it lately,' he said. 'But we've one left.'

He carried it over to the counter for me.

'Mrs Dawson was in here yesterday,' he said. 'We had a very long conversation.'

'Oh?' I replied.

'Yes, she wanted to know where I was from, all the names of my family,' he said. 'She even asked me if I was married.'

'That's Mrs Dawson for you,' I said.

'And the funny thing is,' continued Mr Patel, 'she didn't buy anything.'

'Oh,' I said again, realising that I wasn't being particularly interesting. I yearned to be interesting, to have a deep, meaningful conversation with Mr Patel but all I could think of was 'Oh'.

'Did you hear the fireworks last night?' I asked.

'Yes,' replied Mr Patel. 'They seemed to be coming from the playing fields.'

'They kept Mrs Patel up all night.'

My heart sank. There was a Mrs Patel after all.

'Mrs Patel?' I said.

'My mother,' he replied.

'Oh, I don't think I've seen Mrs Patel before,' I said.

'She doesn't work in the shop,' replied Mr Patel. 'Her English isn't so good.

He smiled.

'I'm sure that she would like to meet you though,' he said.

He produced a loaf of bread and put it beside the Madeira cake.

'For the ducks,' he said. 'It's only 39p today.'

'Thanks, Paul,' I said. It was the first time I'd called him Paul and for a few seconds there seemed to be a recognition, a bond, between us.

'Are you still going to the park on Thursday?' he asked.

'Yes,' I replied. 'About 2 o'clock.'

'I'll see you there,' he said, smiling, 'and at the meeting tomorrow.'

'The meeting?' I asked.

'The meeting at the library to stop its closure,' said Mr Patel, pointing to a notice advertising the event which had been blu-tacked to the wall.

'Mrs Dawson gave me a leaflet yesterday,' he said. 'It's very important. We need our libraries.'

I handed Paul the money for the bread and Madeira cake.

'I'll hopefully see you there,' I said as I turned to leave the shop.

'Bye, Gemma,' he said.

'Bye, Paul,' I replied.

The bell above the door rang twice as I left. I wondered how many thousands of customers that bell had greeted over the years. Mrs Dawson said it dated from, at least, the early 1940s.

I stepped out into the street. The blackbird and the other birds seemed to be singing sweeter than they normally did and I walked with a spring along the wonderful tree lined lanes of Rennie Avenue, along Marsh Road, up Cornwall Street towards Portland Road and through the library doors.

'What a beautiful day,' I announced as I entered.

Miss Taylor eyed me curiously as if I had suddenly gone quite mad. I could see her gaze diverted towards my Madeira cake but I quickly tucked it under my coat, out of sight. Brian and Callum smiled while Cecilia Moorhouse looked as haughty as ever.

'It is indeed a beautiful day,' said Mr Peters, the ends of his moustache looking like they had been freshly waxed. If I ever felt that any of the staff were getting me down, particularly Miss Taylor and Cecilia Moorhouse, Mr Peters was always there to brighten things up.

'He's an eternal optimist,' Mrs Dawson had said. 'And always happy. Maybe you should get a cat like Malcolm.'

I locked my Madeira cake in my locker out of the way of prying hands. As I left the staffroom, Cecilia Moorhouse was showing two zipped-up anorak type people to the reference room.

'We have a large family and local history section,' she announced as they followed her along the hallway.

She looked at me as if to say, 'I'm a proper librarian, you're just a shelf filler.'

Her haughtiness knew no bounds. Even Mr Peters as head of the library was talked down to by Miss Moorhouse. He didn't let it bother him though.

'I'm sure she means well,' he'd said. Mr Peters didn't have a bad word to say about anyone.

Downstairs, Callum told me that Mr Peters was having a meeting of all the staff at 10am.

'It has something to do with the closure of the library,' he said.

'Oh,' I said. 'Will he be wanting tea?'

'I suppose so,' replied Callum as he returned to the children's section with a pile of returned books.

I suddenly felt mean locking my Madeira cake in my locker and decided that I would get it out when we all had tea at 10am and we could all have a bit, even Miss Taylor and Cecilia Moorhouse, although I doubted that Miss Moorhouse ever ate cake; she was rake thin and always wore a tight nylon polo neck jumper which revealed her ribs, together with a tweed skirt which covered her knees. She had the body of an underfed teenage boy and a short, dyed black, bob hairstyle that was last fashionable in the 1960s. Her out of date, pointed in the corner glasses, completed the look.

Mrs Dawson popped into the library at about 9.30am.

'I've finished Rebecca,' she announced. 'It was very good, you should read it.'

Mrs Dawson had read Rebecca at least five times that I knew about.

'Last night I dreamt I went to Manderley again,' said Mrs Dawson.

'Sorry?' I said as I scanned the book.

'It's from the first line of Rebecca,' replied Mrs Dawson.

'Laurence Olivier was in the film,' she continued. 'I didn't care for him much. It was on Channel 4 the other night. Did you see it?'

'No,' I replied.

'Oh,' said Mrs Dawson. 'It was very good. Joan Fontaine played the new Mrs De Winter.'
She looked over to Miss Taylor who was carefully re-arranging the music section.

'That one isn't unlike Mrs Danvers,' said Mrs Dawson nodding towards Miss Taylor. 'Always dressed in black with a cruel streak about her. You'll have to read it, dear. It's wonderful.'
I looked down at the cover and put the book to one side so that I could take it home later. It wasn't the sort of book that I normally read but Mrs Dawson had sold it to me.

'They're having a meeting at ten,' I said. 'Just the staff, about the closure of the library.'

'But we're having our meeting tomorrow,' said Mrs Dawson.

'Maybe it's in preparation for that,' I suggested.

'What's that one done to his moustache?' she said, pointing over towards Mr Peters.

'I think that he's waxed the ends,' I said. 'Rather like Salvador Dali.'

'It looks a bit queer to me,' said Mrs Dawson. 'There used to be a man down at the market with a similar one. That was a very long time ago though.'

'It suits him,' I said.

'He should shave it off,' said Mrs Dawson.

'I don't know,' I said. 'It sort of looks distinguished.'
We both gazed over at Mr Peters until he noticed us staring and we quickly looked away.

'Paul said that he'd be coming tomorrow,' I said.

'Paul?' Mrs Dawson asked.

'Mr Patel from the corner shop,' I continued.

'He's very interested in saving the library.'

'Oh, yes. He's a lovely man,' said Mrs Dawson. 'I had a chat with him yesterday.'

'I know,' I said. 'He told me. I thought that you didn't shop in Patel's?'

'Oh, I didn't buy anything,' said Mrs Dawson. 'His prices are far too high. I just popped in to give him a leaflet and pass the time of day.'

'You asked him if he was married,' I said.

'I was just showing an interest,' said Mrs Dawson. 'He isn't, by the way, he's very much single.'

'Oh,' I replied.

'I just thought that you'd like to know,' she replied.

The other members of staff were beginning to gather around the seated area in front of general non-fiction.

'I bought some Madeira cake for us to eat on Thursday,' I said. 'But I felt a bit selfish so I'm going to give everybody at the meeting a bit with their cups of tea.'

'Including Miss Taylor?' Mrs Dawson asked.

'Yes, including Miss Taylor,' I replied.

Mrs Dawson looked across at the gathering.

'Whatever does he think he looks like with that moustache?' she said before turning to leave. She smiled.

'I'll see you later, dear,' she said. 'I've a bit of shopping to do.'

The morning was pretty quiet with only a few customers coming through our doors, most mainly to get out of the rain. I made the tea in various mugs for the meeting. Everyone had their own mug and woe betide anyone who used the wrong one. Callum's mug had a picture of a scene from Star Wars with the words

May the Force Be With You; Brian's mug had a picture of Alan Titchmarsh; Cecilia's had a painting by Monet on it; Miss Taylor's had a picture of a garden bird, I think, a Goldfinch; Mr Peters' mug had a picture of a curled up cat, fast asleep, which looked just like Malcolm. My mug had the slogan Keep Calm and Carry On. I brought out plates and cut a piece of Madeira cake for everyone.

'Thanks, Gemma,' said Mr Peters. 'That looks lovely.'

Miss Taylor eyed it cautiously before placing it back on the table. Cecilia pulled a face as if she'd never seen anything so common. I handed Callum a piece. Brian mouthed behind him, 'He's diabetic.'

I'm sure that he didn't mean to say the words out loud but he did anyway.

'It's alright,' said Callum. 'My blood sugar is a bit low and I do love a piece of Madeira cake. Thanks.'

Mr Peters shuffled some papers and then looked seriously at us all.

'As you know,' he said. 'The library is due to shut on 22nd June. There's a meeting tomorrow, a coffee morning.'

'A coffee morning?' said Miss Moorhouse, dismissively. 'That will do a lot of good.'

She eyed up the piece of cake that had been cut for her but we both knew that she wasn't about to eat it. In fact, I had never seen Miss Moorhouse ever eat anything which would explain her emaciated 6 stone frame.

'Many of the residents from the local community are coming,' I said. 'As well as members of the press, television and Councillor Evans.'

'Good luck with that,' said Miss Taylor, pulling the sides of her mouth down as far as they would go. I often wondered if they ever stretched in the other direction and produced a smile.

'Will there be cake?' asked Callum.

'Sorry?' I replied.

'Will there be cake at tomorrow's coffee morning?' he repeated. 'I've got to balance my blood sugars and I was just wondering.'
Mr Peters smiled.

'I'm sure that we can supply cake for the handful of people that are expected to turn up,' he said. He looked across at me knowing that I would be the only one to organise it. Neither Miss Taylor or Miss Moorhouse were about to buy cake for their colleagues.

'Well, I think that the whole thing is a complete waste of time,' said Miss Moorhouse.

'We've got to try everything,' replied Mr Peters.

'Well, it won't do any good,' she said, slightly sipping her tea. Her face contorted as if someone had served her yak's urine.

'Is this Earl Grey?' she asked.

'It's PG Tips,' I replied. 'It's all we have.'

'Mrs Dyson has started a petition to keep the library open,' announced Mr Peters, 'and with the newspaper and television coverage as well as local support, we might be able to achieve something.'
The aptly named Mrs Dyson cleaned the library when we all went home. We had all been worried about our jobs but had forgotten about poor Mrs Dyson who would also be unemployed should the library close.

'Who's Mrs Dyson?' asked Miss Taylor which was just the sort of question that Miss Taylor would ask. We all knew who Mrs Dyson was and chatted to her daily but Miss Taylor had never bothered or taken the time to find out anything about Mrs Dyson or her name.

'She works here,' replied Brian, but said no more.

'Is this meeting going to go on for much longer?' asked Miss Taylor. 'Only I've got the music section to sort out. Someone has put many of the books in the wrong places.'
She looked over to me.

'How is one meant to find the book one is looking for when it's filed in the wrong place?' she continued.
She annoyed me immensely every time she said 'one' over and over. I imagined stuffing her uneaten Madeira cake down her throat until she choked on it.

'I just wanted to keep everyone up to date with everything,' said Mr Peters, standing, realising that Miss Taylor was desperate to get off.

'Do you not want your Madeira cake?' I asked. Miss Taylor just said a sharp 'no' and walked off. Miss Moorhouse looked down at the cake and then looked back at me as if I was simple. She said nothing and returned hurriedly to the reference section.

'Do you want another piece of cake?' I asked Callum and Brian. Even with his history of diabetes, Callum refused nothing.

'Gerald Williams will be coming in later to have a good look around,' said Mr Peters. 'The council want to see what they can do with the building once we've gone.'
Mr Peters' words made it all sound far more final.

'What are their plans?' asked Brian.

'Perhaps a community hall or something similar,' replied Mr Peters.

'Aren't we a community hall already,' I said,

'but with books?'

'We'll have to see what happens,' said Mr Peters, looking more than a little fed up.

He got up, half smiled, and returned to the front desk.

In the afternoon, myopic Nigel Wain came into the library, as he did on most days. He seemed to see me clear enough but when reading, he would sit in the corner, at one of the tables with his nose almost touching the newspaper he was reading. He always came in at about 2pm, always smartly dressed, complete with a silk tie and always read The Guardian from cover to cover. He was one of those people that it was difficult to tell their age. He could have been 35 but then again, he could have been 55. His fair hair covered up most of his baldness and his black-rimmed glasses would have fitted in just as well in the 1950s as they did today. He reminded me, to look at, of Noel Gallagher from Oasis. That's not saying that he was cool in any way, he most certainly wasn't. But, then again, maybe he was, in a nerdy sort of Bill Nighy kind of way.

'Hello Gemma,' he said, as I handed him the latest copy of The Guardian. 'There's a slight breeze out there today.'

He'd called me Gemma for several years since we got to know each other when I started making him a cup of coffee to drink with his Guardian. I was just being friendly but the practice was frowned upon by Miss Taylor.

'That coffee is for the staff not the borrowers,' she'd said huffily.

She called everyone who visited the library 'The Borrowers'. I imagined them all returning home to live under someone's floor boards, only coming out to steal small scraps of food.

Just to annoy Miss Taylor, I made sure that I made Nigel a cup of coffee every day and served it to him in a nice china cup with a saucer. On many occasions, I'd given him a couple of digestives, something I also treated Mrs Dawson to, if Miss Taylor was in eyeshot.

'It's not on,' complained Miss Taylor to Mr Peters. 'The coffee is there for the staff not the customers.'

Mr Peters glanced across at Nigel and smiled.

'I can't see what harm it does,' he said. 'We're here to keep everyone happy.'

'We'll be opening a cafe next,' muttered Miss Taylor before she wandered off.

With the closure of the library approaching, maybe a little cafe wouldn't be a bad idea to attract more people in. I decided to suggest it to Mr Peters.

'I see the library is closing down,' Nigel said as I handed him his coffee. 'I got a leaflet through the door about it.'

'There's a meeting tomorrow,' I said.

The traffic coming into the library slowed down in the afternoon. Behind the Women's Health section, Mr Peters, Brian and Callum were giggling away. I could hear them from the Caring For Your Pet section.

They could be like three naughty schoolboys at times. I wasn't sure if I was allowed to join in with their mischief or not but moved in closer with a selection of books as if I was filing them away.

'Wrong,' announced Mr Peters.

Callum looked bemused.

'I'm sure that one was right,' he said.

I moved closer. Mr Peters smiled at me.

'What are you doing?' I asked.

'We're playing William Shakespeare or Charles Dickens,' he said.

'Oh,' I replied. 'How does that work? Can I play?'

I suddenly felt like a child in the school playground.

'Of course you can, Gemma,' said Mr Peters. 'I say a title and you've got to say whether it was written by William Shakespeare or Charles Dickens.'

I thought about it for a couple of seconds. We all worked in a library, surely we all knew the difference between William Shakespeare and Charles Dickens. I glanced at Callum. 'Surely,' I thought.

'Last week we played William Shakespeare or William Shatner,' said Brian.

'How are they even similar?' I asked.

'You'd be surprised,' said Callum, without elaborating any further.

'Okay,' I said. 'Give me a title. I've a feeling I'm going to score 100% at this.'

Mr Peters took a deep breath as if he was preparing himself for something great.

'Right,' he said. 'A Midsummer Night's Dream.'

'Obviously Shakespeare,' I said. 'I don't see the point of this.'

Callum giggled. It was the sort of giggle a three-year-old girl would make if she'd just put a spider in someone's shoe.

'I started with an easy one,' said Mr Peters. 'How about 'All's Well That Ends Well.'

'Dickens?' asked Callum.

'It's Shakespeare,' I said. 'This is a silly game.'

'Our Mutual Friend,' said Mr Peters.

'Dickens,' I said.

'Shakespeare,' said Callum.

Miss Taylor suddenly appeared looking at all four of us like a school teacher who had caught her charges up to no good.

'Shakespeare or Dickens?' Brian asked.

Miss Taylor looked at him with disgust.

'Some of us have work to do,' she said.

She wasn't in charge but liked to put people in their place. It sort of ruined the vibe of the game, not that it was much of a game anyway. We all wandered back to our various sections in the library. Even Mr Peters, although he was still giggling as he left. Perhaps it was a boys' thing.

It seemed forever for five o'clock to come around. I watched the clock slowly ticking away. The second hand seemed to tick even slower than usual. I convinced myself I could stop it ticking just by looking at it.

I headed back home, walking slowly. It was a lovely sunny evening. I smiled to myself as I thought of the 'boys' playing Shakespeare or Dickens although it wasn't really funny at all. I suppose the funny bit had been the look on Miss Taylor's face.

Mr Bishop was busily adjusting the headlights on his car as I passed him.

'Hello, Gemma,' he said. 'Nice evening for it.'

I wasn't sure what 'it' was but he always said the same. He loved that car, always polishing, always cleaning.

I put the key in the door and prepared for a night alone, feet up watching an old film on channel 81. Something about a boy and a unicorn. It all looked a bit corny but I thought I'd watch it anyway.

I wondered how well Mrs Dawson had got on handing out her leaflets. I thought about phoning her but it was getting late by the time I'd had my tea, frozen fish and chips from Patels, and I was sure she was probably very busy, visiting friends or her sister, Alice. I didn't want to disrupt anything and, anyway, the movie really wasn't that bad.

Chapter Eight

Tuesday proved a restless night. There were no more fireworks but the thought of the following morning's meeting went over and over in my head. I imagined a handful of people including Mrs Dawson and Mr Patel turning up and us all sitting in silence, drinking coffee, wondering what to say. I got up at 1am and read a little. Our resident blackbird was happily singing in the background. Like me, he hardly seemed to sleep. I finally dozed off at about 3am but had weird, disturbing dreams. As I slept, I searched the city for Madeira cake but everywhere was closed even Mr Patel's, Miss Taylor was the Child Catcher from Chitty Chitty Bang Bang and rounded up everyone who was opposed to closing the library and, worse still, Mr Patel went off with Cecilia Moorhouse. What would he see in her? By 5am, I was glad to wake up, the image of

Miss Taylor with hollow eyes and a large net still haunting me.

I got up and had some cornflakes at the kitchen table staring out, bleary eyed, towards the street. A spider had spun a web on the outside of the window and waited in the corner of the frame, where there was a small hole, hoping to catch any passing flies. I thought about trying to reach out and knock it down but the spider had put so much work into his ornate web that I decided to leave it alone.

I thought I saw a cat run quickly down the path but as I stared, I realised that it was a fox; very ginger with a big bushy tail. I followed it along the street before it stopped and turned into a narrow alleyway, where it was met by three cubs. I looked up and there was Norman Drudge sat in his window, holding his binoculars. I suddenly realised that it was the fox that he was watching and not the lady at number 10's large chest. If he liked wildlife, I reasoned, he couldn't be all bad. Perhaps the library could be saved after all. I was still half asleep and after Norman disappeared, I left the kitchen table and got ready to meet the day.

It was breezy outside and even though it was the middle of the year, autumn leaves were already blowing off the trees and were swept along the pavement, gathering in a bricked-off area close to the area's only phone box. The box had seen better days; its red paint was flaking off and it had several smashed windows. I couldn't remember the last time I'd seen anyone use it, perhaps it no longer worked. There was a large sign stuck to the window saying that it accepted debit cards and telling passersby that emails could be sent from it but I'd never seen anyone try as everyone nowadays had their own mobile phones. From the smell as I passed, its only use seemed to be as a makeshift toilet. Mr Granger had started a petition to have it removed but few people signed it and, as Mr Bishop pointed out, it was part of our heritage and should remain. He'd even offered to repaint it and tidy it up but the council had never got back to him.

I'd seen a phone box in the town turned into a makeshift library, full of second-hand books which people could leave or take, free of charge. I decided to suggest the idea to Mr Bishop. Perhaps our library could start it off, supplying it with some of our older books. But, I suppose, if the library was soon to close, perhaps there was little point.

Mr Bertram was our resident road sweeper who always complained about the state of the street.

'You would think that people would learn to pick up after themselves,' he'd say. 'There's plenty of bins around.'

We had nearly the same conversation every time we met. Mr Bertram was very short, his head barely reaching the top of his dustcart. I wondered how he managed to get any litter he found into the top of it. Not that it was a good idea to mention his height, or the lack of it. He was particularly sensitive and had a very short fuse. He'd once chased a small boy with his broom when he asked him if he would be appearing in that year's pantomime. I did my best to pretend that I hadn't noticed how short he was although any conversation involved a lot of looking down. I was always careful with what I said, trying my best not to bring the words 'little,' 'tiny' or 'small' into the conversation.

Anyway, Mr Bartram was nowhere in sight today which was just as well. My nerves were already shot without an 'Oompa Loompa' chasing me angrily up and down the street. That's what Mrs Dawson called him, 'Winslow Place's Oompa Loompa.' I don't think that she meant to be unkind, she just got fed up with him blowing his top every time anyone said anything out of turn.

'Is that comment aimed at me?' he'd scowl.

I decided not to go into Mr Patel's on the way to work as, hopefully, I'd be seeing him at the library later and I didn't want to appear too pushy. I strolled along Winslow Place glancing in Mr Patel's window as I passed. It was meant to be just a sideways, unnoticed, glance but Mr Patel Senior saw me and waved.

'Hello, Gemma,' he shouted.
I was surprised that Mr Patel Senior knew my name. Perhaps Paul had been talking about me. I smiled and waved back.

'Hello, Mr Patel,' I said. 'I'm on my way to work.'
Of course he knew that I was on my way to work but I felt that I had to say something and it was all that I could think of.
I carried along to the end of Winslow Place, no Mr Graves today, through Rennie Avenue, along Marsh Road, up Cornwall Street and towards Portland Road. I could hear a lot of noise as I approached the library. Usually things were very quiet at this time of the morning. The closer I got to the library, I could see that there was a noisy commotion outside. A large group of people had gathered, all waving placards and chanting. I thought that there must be some sort of march planned or something, which seemed odd because I didn't know anything about it and I usually knew about every event going on in the area.

As I got closer, I suddenly realised what all the fuss was about. At least forty people stood by the doorway to the building and, as I listened, I could hear them chanting over and over again, 'Save Our Library, Save Our Library'. Some had homemade placards, including ones saying, 'Have A Novel Idea, Save Our Library' and 'A Good Book is Like A Good Friend'.

In the middle of the protest stood Councillor Evans, his nylon shirt buttoned up too tight around his protruding belly. One button had come undone so that his navel was showing. It was quite a hairy navel, not a pretty sight first thing in the morning. Councillor Evans was busily talking to a reporter accompanied by a television crew.

'It's vital that we save our local services,' he said. 'My constituency is all about community. We mustn't let the Conservatives close us down.'

Everyone cheered and continued to chant 'Save Our Library' almost drowning out what Councillor Evans was trying to say.

Mrs Dawson approached me from the crowd.

'Hello, dear,' she said. 'I'm afraid it's all got a bit out of hand. There are even more people inside. The coffee morning has turned into a full blown demonstration.'

'We won't have enough biscuits,' I said, jokingly.

I could see Mr Peters and Norman Drudge waiting to be interviewed by a television reporter. Mr Peters looked very smart today, his moustache waxed at right angles.

'He looks very dapper, doesn't he?' said Mrs Dawson. 'I can see now how that moustache makes him stand out from the crowd. It gives him an air of authority, doesn't it, dear?'

Mr Peters stepped forwards as the television reporter pointed his microphone at him. The microphone was slightly more hairy than Mr Peters' moustache.

'The library obviously has the community's full support, as you can see,' said Mr Peters. 'It's vital that it stays open.'

He looked very passionate, serious and slightly, perhaps, angry. Mr Peters was usually far more mild-mannered.

'The council is committed to amalgamating this library with the Central Library,' said Norman, as the crowd booed his every word.

He looked flustered, I almost felt sorry for him. Almost.

'The decision has been made,' he said. 'The library will close in June.'

People in the crowd pushed and shoved against each other, desperate to hear everything that was going on. There were more boos. Someone made a loud noise with a wooden rattle. It was the sort of rattle that was once popular at football matches in the 1940s. There was an old photo of someone using one kept in the reference section of the library. I don't think that I'd seen or heard one ever. The person holding it looked well into his seventies.

'Norman looks a lot shorter in real life,' said Mrs Dawson, even though she'd already seen him in 'real life' in the library.

It was an odd thing to say but I suppose seeing him across the way most of the time, in his window, somehow, made him appear taller.

'He hasn't been watching the woman with the large chest,' I said. 'There are a family of foxes living in the alleyway opposite his house.'

Mrs Dawson wasn't convinced.

'It was probably her large chest that got him looking that way in the first place,' she said. 'I know what men are like, that's all they think about.'

Was she referring to her Alf, I wondered, or just men in general?

I looked around the crowd to see who I recognised. I could see Brian and Callum as well as Miss Taylor and Cecilia Moorhouse, looking slightly uncomfortable amongst the large gathering of baying protesters, all jostling, trying to get the best position to see what was going on.

'Have you seen Mr Patel?' I asked Mrs Dawson. 'He said that he was coming.'

'No, dear,' she replied. 'He may be inside. He wasn't in the shop this morning.'

'I thought that you didn't shop in Patel's,' I said. 'After the Shreddies incident.'

'Oh no, I don't,' replied Mrs Dawson. 'I was just looking around.'

Mrs Dawson looked over to the reporter interviewing Mr Peters.

'I wonder if we'll be on the television tonight,' she asked. 'I should have worn something a bit smarter.'

'We'll only be faces in the background,' I said, 'and perhaps it won't be on the telly anyway. I suppose it's not very exciting news. Who's interested in a library closure?'

'Well these people are,' replied Mrs Dawson, as she straightened her top and gave a false smile as the camera panned around the crowd.

Councillor Evans and Norman Drudge caught each other's eye. There was a clear animosity between them.

Evans had always been a Labour man, fighting for workers' rights, a union man, where as Drudge, Gerald Williams, was a staunch Conservative. They were much the same really, working for the council albeit on different sides. Evans dreamt of being a politician, an MP, Prime Minister even, but the calling never came, not that he'd have been up to it anyway.

People started chanting 'Save our library' over and over, increasing in loudness until their voices became deafening.

'Shall we make our way inside?' asked Mrs Dawson. 'It's a bit too busy out here for my liking.'

She grasped me by my hand and led me through the crowd towards the library's doorway, regularly saying 'excuse me, please' as loudly and as forcefully as she could. I think that I knocked shoulders with Norman and although we both whispered a quiet 'sorry' I didn't look back. I was glad to get inside, away from the noise and commotion outside. The busy throng of people that had been inside were now outside joining in the protest. The peace of the library was almost blissful.

'I suppose the coffee morning is off,' said Mrs Dawson. 'I'd bought a packet of Rich Tea biscuits too.'

'We could still have a cup of coffee, I suppose,' I said as I walked over to the area I'd set up for the meeting and switched on the kettle.

'We've only got instant,' I said, taking the jar of Nescafé, with its coffee-encrusted lid, off the shelf and showing it to Mrs Dawson. She looked at the unappealing jar and gave it a look of disdain.

'I know it's a coffee morning,' she said, 'but could I have a cup of tea instead?'

I smiled.

'We've only got teabags,' I said.

Mrs Dawson looked over to the large red box of teabags sitting on the shelf.

'Needs must,' she replied as I reached up and brought down the cup and saucer I kept for 'special' visitors. I got down my 'builder's mug', the one with 'Keep Calm' written on it, and placed it beside the china cup and waited for the kettle to boil. Mrs Dyson always re-washed our cups, even if they were already clean, and placed them tidily on the shelf before she went home. Cecilia Moorhouse never washed her cup and just left it in the sink, knowing that someone else would eventually do it for her. It had a brown stain inside, the result of years of cups of tea that even Mrs Dyson's endless scrubbing couldn't remove.

'I'll have to bring in a Steradent for that,' she'd once said.

One cup I'd never use, even if mine was somehow broken, was Miss Moorhouse's and the thought of Mrs Dyson using the same tablets to clean it that she used to clean her false teeth, made it even less appealing.

The kettle boiled and I poured the hot water into our cups before dipping one of the teabags, that I'd bought in a box of 180 from Mr Patel's, in the water and then adding milk straight from a '4 litres' plastic bottle. Mrs Dawson watched me intently as if I was committing a cardinal sin.

'They were only 49p,' I said. 'For 180.'

'I suppose it's all Miss Taylor deserves,' said Mrs Dawson as she sipped the tea slowly.

'Mr Johnson came around yesterday evening,' said Mrs Dawson.

'Oh,' I said.

'Only he's decided to go and live with his daughter,' said Mrs Dawson, 'in Blackpool.'

'Oh, that's a shame,' I said. 'You got on so well.'

'I know, dear,' replied Mrs Dawson. 'He said that I could go and visit but it's not the same, is it?'

'Blackpool looks okay,' I said. 'It might be nice for a holiday.'

'It's a bit tacky for me,' said Mrs Dawson. 'All trams, sticks of rock and Kiss Me Quick hats. I don't think it's for me. And anyway, it's too far on my own.'

'I could come with you,' I suggested.

'Maybe,' said Mrs Dawson. 'I suppose that would make it a lot more fun.'

I'd only ever seen Blackpool on the television, all bright lights and slot machines. I hadn't played on a slot machine since I was little when my parents had taken me on holiday to Clacton as a small girl. It rained most of the time and we came home early. Mr Peters said that Blackpool was Britain's answer to Las Vegas, not that he'd been to either.

I could see that Mrs Dawson was down in the dumps about Mr Johnson's decision to go and live in Blackpool. Not only had she lost a friend, she'd also lost a dancing partner, someone to go to the cinema with and someone to go on long walks with on Sunday afternoons when she wasn't visiting her sister, Alice.

'Of course he wasn't like Alf,' continued Mrs Dawson. 'No-one could replace Alf.'

We sipped our tea. Mrs Dawson's face grimaced as she drank it.

'You've always got me,' I said. 'We can do all the things that you used to do with Mr Johnson.'

'Of course we can,' she said, cheering up slightly. 'That would be lovely.'

She took a long look around the empty library. The clock's loud tick echoed around the building.

'It would have been Alf and mine's fiftieth wedding anniversary today,' said Mrs Dawson, looking slightly sad.

'I'm sorry I didn't know,' I said, not knowing what to say to comfort her.

I took her hand and rubbed it gently.

'I do miss him,' she said. 'Fifty years is a long time, isn't it, dear?'

'Would you like to go out somewhere?' I asked. 'Perhaps do something different for a change. We could go for a meal, maybe.'

I could see that she needed cheering up.

'No, it's alright, dear,' replied Mrs Dawson, pointing to her heart. 'I'll always have him here. He was something special, you know. I wish you could have met him. I know that I talk a lot about him and he somehow just sounds ordinary, even boring, but he wasn't like that at all. We did have some fun and he did make me laugh. No-one could make me laugh like Alf could.'

I didn't really know what to say so I smiled and sipped my tea. What could I say that would make her feel any better? Sometimes, silence seemed the best option. I continued to drink my tea. Mrs Dawson was right, the cheap stuff wasn't a patch on the tea that we drank on Thursday mornings at my flat.

'I don't think things have been the same since Alf went,' said Mrs Dawson. 'I don't suppose that they ever will be.'

Mrs Dawson stared into space for a few seconds as if reflecting on her past, a past she could never get back.

'I can't imagine that it will do any good,' she continued, changing the subject. 'The protest, that is. I remember when Alf joined a strike, he didn't get paid for four weeks and it didn't achieve anything.'

I couldn't imagine Mrs Dawson's Alf on strike, waving a placard around. Did rat catchers even go on strike, I wondered? I suppose they must have.

'I'll show you the foxes when you come around tomorrow,' I said, 'the ones that Norman was watching.'

'Lovely, I'd like that,' said Mrs Dawson, staring down into her cup of tea, as if the solution to all her problems lay within that cup.

'We used to have foxes in the garden,' she continued. 'They'd come in most days. Alf discovered that they were partial to lasagne.'

'That seems an odd thing to feed them,' I said.

'Alf wasn't partial to pasta or anything Italian,' said Mrs Dawson. 'He was old fashioned, he liked a Sunday roast. He couldn't stand pizza. Freddie Fox got that too.'

I blew on my tea and took a sip. The cheap tea didn't taste unlike pencils. I decided to try Mr Patel's 99p specials next time instead.

'Norman's speech didn't go down too well, did it?' I said. 'He seems a lonely sort of person, doesn't he? Always sat in his window, always staring out on to the street.'

Mrs Dawson thought about what I'd said for a few seconds as she stared down at her tea wondering if it was worth taking another sip.

'Aren't we all,' she said. 'Lonely, that is.'

'There's Mr Peters, him with the funny moustache, with only Malcolm for company,' she continued, 'Brian and Callum don't seem to have any partners and I'm sure that the two Misses, Taylor and Moorhouse, don't have much of a life.'

'I suppose not,' I said.

'And then there's you and me,' said Mrs Dawson. 'I'm a widower and you're on your own.'
I half smiled.

'We've got each other,' I said.

'I won't be around forever,' said Mrs Dawson. 'It makes you think though, doesn't it, dear? We're all lonely in one way or another.'

'I suppose so,' I said, feeling slightly more miserable than I had been when I turned up for work.

'That's why we need places like this,' said Mrs Dawson. 'For the sense of community, where lonely people can meet up, read a book and have a chat.'
She took another sip of her tea before abandoning it completely. She picked up the box of teabags and stared at it intently.

'I wonder who buys this stuff?' she said. 'It's hardly like tea at all.'
I stood up.

'Another cup?' I asked holding up the kettle.
Mrs Dawson eyed her half-finished cup of tea.

'I should really be getting off,' she said. 'Shopping to do and such like.'
I looked quickly around the library. Most of the people who had come for the meeting had either left or joined the crowd outside.

'I thought that Mr Patel would have shown up,' I said.

'Shopkeepers are very busy,' replied Mrs Dawson. 'Especially Indian ones.'

'I suppose so,' I said. 'But he did say that he'd come.'

'Maybe something came up,' said Mrs Dawson. 'Maybe he had a run on those 49p teabags and had to get in new stock.'

I realised she was joking and I half smiled.

'Perhaps he was just being polite,' I said. 'He's probably the same with all his customers.'

Mrs Dawson gazed around the now empty library with its many well-read books and randomly blu-tacked notices on the wall advertising everything from yoga classes to IT for beginners.

'I'll miss this place,' she said. 'It's almost like a second home. A home for wayward spirits who have nowhere else to go.'

I knew what she meant. My life was the library, as well as the charity shop, Mrs Dawson and visits to the park and Mr Patel's. Not that I was unhappy with my lot. I always had my books which kept me occupied on cold, wet days when I couldn't get out or during nights when I couldn't sleep.

'Did you hear the fireworks?' I asked.

'I did,' replied Mrs Dawson. 'It will be kids no doubt. You'd think that their parents would keep them in check. That's the trouble, there's no discipline nowadays. Children are allowed to do whatever they want, running amok, scaring old aged pensioners and the like.'

'It would have scared the foxes too,' I said.

Mrs Dawson got to her feet.

'I suppose I'd better get my shopping,' she said. 'I want to get some Salad Cream before they change it's name.'

'They're changing it's name?' I asked, not that I particularly liked Salad Cream.

'They're changing it to Sandwich Cream,' said Mrs Dawson. 'Have you ever heard anything so daft?'

'Oh,' I said. 'I suppose it will still taste the same though. Won't it?'

'I don't know, dear. They've got to mess around with everything nowadays,' replied Mrs Dawson. 'Why can't they just leave things the way they've always been?'

'Will I see you tomorrow?' I asked. 'For our morning tea?'

'Of course, dear,' Mrs Dawson replied. 'I wouldn't miss it. But get some of that proper tea.' She smiled, got her bags together and walked towards the exit. I watched her disappear out of the non-automatic automatic doors. I was soon all alone in the library, it seemed a big, open lonely place when it was empty. It didn't last long and a couple of minutes later, people started heading in, looking for new books, desperate to get back to normal, after the commotion outside had died down.

Chapter Nine

The resident blackbird woke me on Thursday morning with its beautiful song, happily singing its heart out. I switched my alarm clock off. I never needed it as I always woke up before it went off. Even so, I still set it every evening, knowing that I probably would never hear it ring. Thursday's were always much the same. On my day off, Mrs Dawson would come around in the morning, I'd read a bit, go for a walk in the park in the afternoon and do a bit of shopping before I returned home and read a bit more or watched the television, if there was anything good on.

I had my breakfast, a bowl of Special K, and stared bleary eyed out of the kitchen window. There was no Norman today. Unlike me, he didn't have Thursdays off and had already set off for work. Mr Bishop was busy polishing his Ford Anglia which already gleamed in the sunlight. The dustbin men arrived, clattering about, pushing wheelie bins noisily towards their van before tipping the rubbish into it. I recognised Alan Cole who worked for the refuse team. He was bald-headed, covered in tattoos and had a gold earring in his left ear. His face always looked like it needed a shave, he had a scruffy, filthy look. He was a sort of a cousin but sort of wasn't. My gran and his gran had been sisters or cousins or something similar. He'd turned up one day at the library with a copy of his family tree and said that we must get together sometime. We never did. I wondered as I watched him if he knew that he collected rubbish from my street. I certainly didn't want him to know where I lived, his 'Cockney charm' and grating voice soon wore thin with me, even if we were relations.

Mr Patel made his way past the sprawl of abandoned wheelie bins heading quickly towards his shop. He looked happy enough although the dustbin men took no notice of him. I needed bread but decided not to visit Mr Patel's after he didn't turn up at the library yesterday. I didn't want to appear desperate.

Mrs Dawson arrived at 9.30am. I already had the kettle on. Mrs Dawson always arrived at 9.30am on the dot. She was nothing if not punctual. She sat down at the kitchen table, taking off her fur collar coat and putting it on the back of the chair, tidily, before setting her shopping bags down nearby against the cupboard where I kept all my cleaning stuff, cloths, window cleaner, polish and such like.

'I bought you some bread,' she said. 'For the ducks. I thought that you might not want to go into Mr

Patel's today.'

I felt foolish avoiding Mr Patel because he didn't turn up at the library the day before but Mrs Dawson knew me well enough to buy bread knowing how I'd feel.

'I'm sure he was just busy,' I said. 'I saw him walking down the street this morning, dodging the dustbin men.'

'Oh,' said Mrs Dawson. 'Did you see that awful Alan Cole, the one who claims to be your cousin?'

'Yes, I saw him,' I said. 'He always has that same checked red shirt on and those filthy torn jeans.'

'I'm sure there's a bit of gypsy in him,' said Mrs Dawson. 'Promise me you won't have him in the house, dear.'

I'm not sure if she had an aversion to gypsies or just Alan Cole in particular. Anyway, I wasn't about to make him a cup of tea.

'He has a look of a young Omar Sharif,' said Mrs Dawson suddenly.

'Alan Cole?' I asked.

'No, dear,' replied Mrs Dawson. 'Mr Patel. He has a look of Omar Sharif in Doctor Zhivago. It was on channel 81 the other evening. It was awfully sad.'

I wasn't sure that Mr Patel looked anything like Omar Sharif.

'Is Omar Sharif Indian?' I asked.

'He's something foreign,' replied Mrs Dawson. 'I think he's Egyptian. He likes to gamble, playing cards and such like. Does Mr Patel like playing cards?'

It seemed an odd question. How would I know if Mr Patel played cards?

'I'll ask him next time I'm in his shop,' I joked, as I poured out the tea into our china cups.

Mrs Dawson smiled.

'That looks nicer than the library stuff,' she said as I added a dash of milk. 'Do you think Mr Patel will turn up at the park later?'

'I don't know,' I replied. 'He's probably forgotten.'

Mrs Dawson sipped her tea.

'I might see you there,' she said. 'Just so you're not on your own.'

Mrs Dawson leaned down and pulled the local newspaper out of her bag.

'There's a nice photo of Mr Peters on the front page,' she said.

I stared at the newspaper and the story which appeared under the headline, 'Library To Close.' The photo showed Mr Peters shaking hands with Councillor Evans surrounded by people waving signs and looking generally disgruntled. Miss Taylor looked particularly stern to the left of the picture.

'Is that us disappearing into the library?' I said, pointing to the backs of two figures at the entrance.

'I don't know,' said Mrs Dawson, as she took the paper and squinted closely at the photo.

She reached into her handbag and pulled out her reading glasses and put them on.

'Yes, I believe it is. Fame at last,' she said.

Mrs Dawson stared at the photo for several seconds longer, scrutinising every detail.

'I think that it's time I got a new coat,' she said. 'And perhaps lost a few pounds. There's a wonderful diet in the paper, you just have to stay off carrots.'

'Carrots?' I said. 'That should be easy.'

She flicked through the pages of the newspaper and laughed.

'Sorry, dear,' she said. 'It's not carrots, it's

carbohydrates. I really need to get a new pair of glasses.'

'I'm not even sure what a carbohydrate is,' I said.

'Nor do I,' said Mrs Dawson, continuing to read the paper, 'but they're bad for you anyway.'
I lifted up the loaf of bread that Mrs Dawson bought, got up, and headed for the grill.

'Fancy some toast?' I said changing the subject. 'I've got some nice marmalade.'

'Is it Robertson's?' Mrs Dawson asked.

'I don't know,' I replied handing her the jar.
She studied it carefully, looking slightly disgruntled as she examined it.

'Sureena?' said Mrs Dawson. 'I haven't heard of this make.'

'It's from Mr Patel's,' I said. 'It's very cheap.'
She put the jar back down on the table as if she was dismissing it.

'Alf used to like Robertson's marmalade on his toast before he went to work,' said Mrs Dawson. 'There used to be a golliwog on the side of the jar. I haven't seen one of those for a long time.'
I opened the loaf of bread and popped a couple of slices into the toaster. I decided not to use the grill. It tasted better that way but the toaster was far more convenient and quicker.

'I'm sure the ducks won't miss it,' I said.
Mrs Dawson took off her reading glasses which had been balanced on the end of her nose and replaced them in a green case which she put back in her handbag.

'I did enjoy that Black and White Minstrels record you gave me,' said Mrs Dawson. 'Stop your ticklin', Jock was a particular favourite of Alf and me. I remember it on the television. Minstrels dressed in kilts with bright ginger hair.'

It sounded a very odd type of programme to me.

The toast popped up and I took it out and spread some 'Sureena' margarine on it before adding the marmalade and placing it on a fine china plate and handing it to Mrs Dawson.

'Of course they wouldn't allow any of it today,' she said. 'But we did enjoy it at the time. I saw the Minstrels at The Pavilion. I suppose it must have been in about 1978.'

I took a bite of my toast as I read the newspaper article. Mrs Dawson was right, Robertson's marmalade was better and, although not healthy, I decided to buy butter in future.

'The article quotes Councillor Evans as saying there's a very good chance, with the support of the community,' I said, 'that the library will stay open.'

Mrs Dawson grimaced.

'He'll say anything to get his face in the paper,' she said. 'You know what he's like.'

Mrs Dawson gingerly ate her toast as if she'd never tasted anything quite like it before. I wasn't sure if she was enjoying it or not but I assumed that she wasn't.

'I'll see what Mr Peters has to say tomorrow,' I said.

'What we need is another protest,' said Mrs Dawson. 'Something larger, perhaps outside the Guildhall.'

Later in the afternoon, I found myself, sitting alone, on my favourite bench in the park looking across the pond, with Mrs Dawson's loaf of bread beside me. It was particularly quiet with not a duck in sight.

'Hello, Gemma,' a voice said from behind. I jumped and turned to see who it was. It was Mr Patel.

'I didn't mean to startle you,' he said.

He was carrying a bunch of flowers which I recognised from the shop - £3.99 reduced to £2.99.

'These are for you,' he said.

I smiled, no-one had ever given me flowers before. They were very colourful almost like someone had dyed them bright blues, yellows and reds.

'Thanks,' I said. 'They're lovely.'

'May I sit down?' Mr Patel asked.

'Of course,' I said, lifting the loaf of bread and budging up a bit.

Mr Patel sat beside me staring out to the pond.

'No ducks today,' he said.

'No,' I replied.

He picked up the loaf of bread.

'This will be why,' he joked. 'They only like bread from Patel's.'

He broke off a bit and chucked it in the direction of the pond. As he did so, a duck swooped down to eat it.

'They're always around, always watching,' he said. 'Even when you can't see them.'

We both broke off pieces of bread and threw them in the direction of the pond as more ducks flocked around to eat it. Several came out of the water and one pecked at Mr Patel's shoe.

'They seem to like you,' I said.

He smiled.

'They know that I'm the person who sells the bread,' he joked.

It was nice to have company, male company. I looked around for Mrs Dawson who was normally in the park at this time but couldn't see her anywhere.

'I'm sorry I missed your meeting yesterday,' said Mr Patel.

'That's fine,' I said. 'Lots of people turned up, it's in today's paper.'

'I saw it,' Mr Patel replied. 'We sell it in the shop.'

'I don't suppose it will do any good anyway,' I said. 'I don't suppose there's much that can be done to stop the library's closure now.'

'But, it's part of the community,' said Mr Patel. 'It needs saving.'

'Mrs Dawson wants to organise a protest at the Guildhall,' I said.

The duck continued to bite Mr Patel's shoe and he broke off more bread and fed it to it.

'He's a cheeky devil,' he said.

I thought I caught a glimpse of Mrs Dawson walking the other way in the distance. I couldn't be sure though, there were lots of elderly women with fur-collared coats in the park.

'I'm sorry I missed the protest,' said Mr Patel. 'I had to take Mrs Patel to the hospital.'

It seemed odd that he would call his mother 'Mrs Patel'.

'Is she alright?' I asked.

'She tripped and fell over a box of Custard Creams,' he said. 'She's quite a woman but they broke her fall.'

By 'quite a woman' I assumed he meant overweight.

'Was there any damage?' I asked.

'We've opened a broken biscuit section,' he joked. '50p a bag.'

'Mrs Dawson will like that,' I said. 'She's always telling me how the shops used to sell broken biscuits.'

A duck leapt on the bench beside us. I jumped.

'Mrs Patel is fine. She's taking it easy in bed, just a sprained ankle,' said Mr Patel, shooing away the duck carefully. 'We had to sit up in A&E for six hours.' I picked up the flowers and breathed in their aroma. They seemed to have a strange toffee popcorn sort of smell. It was a smell that I'd only experienced in the local cinema.

'They really are lovely,' I said.

'They're just from the shop,' said Mr Patel. 'Two for £4.99.'

He smiled.

'Would you like to go for a walk?' he asked. 'We could walk around the pond.'

We got up, the ducks seemed disappointed that we were leaving. Mr Patel broke up the rest of the bread and scattered it around as the ducks fought over it. It seemed odd strolling around the park with Mr Patel. I realised that I needed to stop thinking of him as 'Mr Patel' and start thinking of him as 'Paul'. Mr Patel was far too formal.

'My mother said that I should ask you around for tea tomorrow,' said Paul. 'That's if you would like to come.'

'I'd love to,' I said, realising that I knew nothing about Indian traditions or food. What if Mrs Patel made something I didn't like or recognise? What would I wear? In times like this, my mind went into overdrive and anxiety set in. Maybe I shouldn't have said 'yes' but I wanted to go, so of course, I should have said yes. Nerves always got the better of me. I was never a 'joiner in', as my mother had often said. I remembered a school trip to the zoo when I was seven but I was too shy to go so stayed behind, on my own in the classroom, telling the teacher that my mother couldn't afford to let me go. Shyness and anxiety had been the bane of my life.

Since I'd moved to London, I'd decided to grab every opportunity that arose but turning over a new leaf, changing my personality and defeating anxiety and shyness weren't an easy thing. Not that any opportunities arose anyway, until now. Yes, I would go to tea at Mr Patel's.

'Hello, you two,' said a voice from behind. It was Mrs Dawson.

I was glad to see her. I always felt awkward making conversation with new people and a third person, who was happy to talk, helped greatly.

'Hello, Mrs Dawson,' Paul said before I could say anything.

I think that Mrs Dawson was surprised that Paul knew her name although she had been firing questions at him and his family for the last week so how could he forget? I imagined her shining a light in his face rather like the Gestapo interrogating an English spy in one of those old war films on channel 81.

'It's a beautiful day,' said Mrs Dawson. 'The birds are busily chatting away. I saw two greenfinches earlier.'

'It's wonderful,' I replied.

'My Alf and I used to love strolling around this park,' she said. 'When he was alive, of course.'

It seemed a funny thing to say. Of course Mrs Dawson didn't come to the park with her dead husband.

Mrs Dawson looked Paul up and down. I'd never seen her scrutinise someone so much. Paul noticed but politely looked away and pretended he was watching the ducks.

She leaned closer to me.

'He's quite handsome, isn't he?' she whispered. 'He has a look of a young Buddy Holly.'

She raised her voice slightly.

'Anyway, dear, I must get off, shopping to do,' she said. 'I thought that I'd try the new Waitrose.'

'Waitrose? They're very expensive,' said Paul. 'Patel's has everything you could need.'

Mrs Dawson thought back to her out of date Shreddies.

'Anyway, I'm sure I'll see you both soon,' she said.

'Come in the library tomorrow,' I said. 'For a chat. Friday's are always very quiet in the library and I'll let you know if there's any news about the closure.'

'It's a date,' Mrs Dawson joked and headed off to get her shopping.

'I'm not sure that Mrs Dawson likes me,' said Paul as he watched her disappear.

'Oh, she likes you,' I said. 'I can tell. She's like that with everyone at first.'

A lone duck had followed us from the pond and was busily pecking at Paul's heel.

'He wants more bread,' he said as he softly shooed him away.

'What will we have to eat,' I asked, 'when I come round for tea?'

I had to ask. 'Be prepared' Mrs Dawson always said. Paul looked down towards our feathered friend happily pecking at his ankle.

'Duck?' he said.

Chapter Ten

I slept lightly all Thursday night. I'd read a bit before going to bed but, unable to concentrate, I gave up. The flat seemed unusually quiet and lonely. Usually, I was quite happy with my own company either watching an old film on the television or reading a new book. Images of Paul and I walking through the park, Mrs Dawson talking about Buddy Holly, tea at the Patels' and the library closure kept rushing through my head. I was normally a calm person but once I became anxious, it took a while for me to return to normal. I thought of phoning Mrs Dawson but, of course, she was probably fast asleep in bed.

'My Alf used to get like you,' Mrs Dawson had once said to me when I got myself upset after arguing with one of the neighbours. 'It turned out he had a dodgy thyroid. You should get yours checked.'

Mr Barton was particularly annoying, always upsetting

someone with his nonsense.

'He's best ignored,' Mrs Dawson had said at the time and, of course, she was right.

I was up long before I was usually, had my breakfast, watched Norman looking through his binoculars and Mr Bishop polish his car in between staring into a bowl of cornflakes wondering what the day held for me. My blackbird cheerily twittered on my window ledge watching me slowly eat my breakfast.

I left the flat at 8.30am and walked the length of Winslow Place, looking over to Patel's as I passed the end of the street. I couldn't see Paul and decided not to venture into the shop. He wouldn't want to see me bleary eyed, looking half-dead, would he? Perhaps he wouldn't mind, he probably wouldn't, but I felt too edgy through lack of sleep and decided to carry on my way to work. I'd see Paul later for tea, hopefully I'd be more awake by then. I continued along Rennie Avenue, through Marsh Road, up Cornwall Street and Portland Road into the library, hardly noticing my surroundings on the way.

Two men in white overalls were busy adjusting the automatic doors at the entrance of the library when I got there. One tightly held onto a precarious, thin metal stepladder while the other balanced on top adjusting something above his head as the ladder wobbled slightly. I thought about saying 'hello' but I didn't want to distract them from their work and gave them plenty of room as I walked by, not wanting to unwittingly nudge them and cause some hideous accident. The library already had enough problems without a claim for compensation.

Miss Taylor was milling about behind the front desk when I arrived. She saw me enter, looked my way, checked her watch and then looked at the clock. I wasn't late but it was a procedure she went through every morning. I scowled at her. I was normally friendly but Miss Taylor's continual harassment was starting to wear thin.

'Better late than never,' she said, in earshot of Mr Peters.

'At least I don't live here,' I said. 'Some of us actually have a life.'

Miss Taylor looked shocked.

'Perhaps if you tried being less of a cow,' I said, 'the day would pass a lot quicker.'

It wasn't in my personality to be nasty to people but Miss Taylor had been asking for it for years. I suddenly felt a lot better putting her in her place. I was going to say more but then, totally unexpected, Miss Taylor burst into tears, dropped the books she had been collecting and fled to the staffroom.

'Oh dear,' said Mr Peters.

He didn't like Miss Taylor any more than I did but he was in charge and felt he should do something.

'Oh dear,' he said again.

I picked up the books dropped by Miss Taylor and put them on the side.

'I'm not apologising,' I said. 'I've had just about all I'm going to take from that woman.'

Mr Peters was clearly shocked, he'd never seen me anything other than quiet and easygoing. I didn't even know why I was in a bad mood but I knew that today, of all days, I wasn't about to put up with rudeness from anyone.

'I realise that Miss Taylor is an acquired taste,' said Mr Peters, 'but we've all got to try and knock along together.'

He gazed in the general direction of the staffroom. Secretly, he was a little scared of the overbearing Miss Taylor.

'I suppose I should go and see if she's alright,' he said.

'I'm not apologising,' I said, as Mr Peters left for the staffroom.

I didn't see Miss Taylor for the rest of the morning. I planned on ignoring her even if she did show her face but she kept well out of the way.

Mrs Dawson arrived at 10am.

'It's quiet in here today, dear,' she said. 'Has someone died?'

'I've had a row with Miss Taylor,' I said. 'I'm not apologising.'

Mrs Dawson looked around the library.

'I'm sure she deserved it,' she said. 'She can be a right cow at the best of times. Where is she now?'

'Crying in the staffroom, probably' I said. 'Pouring out all her problems to Mr Peters.'

Mrs Dawson reached into her handbag.

'I bought you something,' she said. 'A present.' She handed me a nicely wrapped package covered in a flower patterned print paper, tied up with a red ribbon. A little red bow was stuck in the corner.

'That's lovely, thank you,' I said. 'Is it a book?'

'Yes,' said Mrs Dawson. 'But open it later, when you're on your own and haven't had a row with Miss Taylor.'

'It's very kind,' I said, carefully placing the book in my bag.

'How did you get on with Mr Patel yesterday?' asked Mrs Dawson.

'We walked around the park, fed the ducks,

talked a bit and then he walked me home,' I said.

'And?' asked Mrs Dawson.

'That was it,' I replied.

'You didn't asked him in for a cup of tea?' asked Mrs Dawson.

'No,' I replied. 'I didn't want to appear too forward.'

'Oh,' replied Mrs Dawson.

'I ran upstairs and watched him walk back to his shop though,' I said. 'I haven't seen him today.'

'Oh,' said Mrs Dawson, keeping one eye on the staffroom to see if Miss Taylor was re-appearing.

'I didn't sleep at all,' I said. 'And I'm supposed to go to the Patels' for tea this evening. What will I wear?'

'Just go as yourself, dear,' said Mrs Dawson. 'Just dress as you do normally. I'm sure that's what Mr Patel loves you for.'

'Mr Patel doesn't love me,' I said, blushing. He didn't, did he?

'Well, he certainly seems interested,' said Mrs Dawson.

In the distance, I could see that Miss Taylor had re-emerged from the staffroom. Mrs Dawson followed my eye line towards her.

'Just ignore her, dear,' she said.

'I'm not sure I should go,' I said. 'To Mr Patel's, that is.'

'Why ever not?' asked Mrs Dawson.

'I've worked myself up too much about it now,' I said. 'I just feel uncomfortable and edgy. I think that I prefer my quiet life, no complications, every day the same.'

'You won't meet anyone like that,' said Mrs

Dawson.

She was right but I'd got used to just working at the library, meeting up with Mrs Dawson, reading books, feeding the ducks and generally being on my own. Now Mr Patel had been thrown into the mix and upset everything.

'Look at me with Miss Taylor,' I said. 'I never usually argue with anyone.'

'She deserves it,' said Mrs Dawson.

'But I don't really know her,' I said. 'Perhaps she's got a really miserable home life and now I've been horrible to her and made her cry. I feel awful.'

'I suppose,' said Mrs Dawson. 'But don't go blaming yourself. Look how many people that she's upset over the years.'

I did feel guilty though. Miss Taylor was unpleasant but no more unpleasant than Cecilia Moorhouse.

'Should I apologise?' I asked.

'No you certainly shouldn't,' replied Mrs Dawson. 'Let her think for a while about how she treats other people. It will do her good.'

Mr Peters sidled up beside me and scanned some returned books. Mrs Dawson seemed fascinated by his moustache which, today, was sort of knitted into pigtails at each end.

'How's Miss Taylor?' I asked.

'She seems alright now. She was a bit upset,' said Mr Peters. 'I know that she can be very trying at times.'

I felt guilty.

'Should I speak to her,' I asked. 'Should I apologise?'

Mr Peters was about to say something but was interrupted by Mrs Dawson.

'You've got nothing to apologise for,' she said. 'That woman has been horrible to you.'

I noticed Miss Taylor look over at us, huddled together, talking. I felt sure that she would be thinking that we were talking about her which, of course, we were. I suddenly felt sorry for her. The more we talked, the more uncomfortable I felt. My head had been spinning all morning, worrying about it.

'I feel unwell,' I said. 'Can I go home?'

'Whatever's the matter, dear?' asked Mrs Dawson.

'You know,' I replied. Only Mrs Dawson didn't know.

'It's everything,' I said. 'Can I go home, please?'

Mr Peters called Callum over from the children's section.

'Gemma's feeling unwell,' he said. 'She's going to take the afternoon off. Could you take over the desk?'

Callum looked at me and nodded without saying anything. Perhaps he thought that I was going to shout at him also if he said a wrong word. What had I turned into?

'I feel like I'm letting everyone down,' I said.

'You're not letting anyone down,' said Mrs Dawson.

Mr Peters smiled.

'It's fine, Gemma,' he said. 'Go home and take it easy and we'll see you again on Monday. And don't go worrying about Miss Taylor.'

Only I did worry about Miss Taylor and everything else that was going on in my life at the moment.

Chapter Eleven

Mrs Dawson walked me back home from the library. I hardly remembered walking along Portland Road, Cornwall Street, Marsh Road, Rennie Avenue, or home to Winslow Place. The whole journey just merged into one blurry mess. I could feel a headache coming on.

I lay on the couch as Mrs Dawson made me a cup of tea.

'It will be a migraine,' she said. 'Alf used to get them all the time. It was brought on by stress. He nearly had a breakdown at Eagle Insurance.'

Alf had worked at Eagle Insurance for a couple of years when they first married but the pressure became too much and he left and joined the council. Working outdoors 'relaxed his nerves', Mrs Dawson had once said.

The kettle boiled and I heard Mrs Dawson pouring the

water into the teapot. It all sounded very loud today. I just wanted to lie down in a darkened room and hopefully go to sleep.

'Chocolate used to bring it on. So did coffee,' said Mrs Dawson. 'Tomatoes didn't agree with him much either.'

I sat up and looked around the room. The light was bright and my eyes were strangely out of focus with zigzaggy lines in front of them. I thought about calling the doctor but no, he'd just dismiss my symptoms as he always did. Dr McColl's answer to any illness was to prescribe anti-depressants and I wasn't about to take them. Mrs Dawson said that her Alice had been like a zombie on them.

I closed my eyes for a few seconds, hoping that things, especially my vision, would calm down. It made little difference.

'Do you think that you could tell Paul,' I said, 'that I won't be coming.'

Mrs Dawson poured the tea into our favourite china cups.

'Are you sure?' she said. 'You might be better by this evening.'

I wasn't sure. I wanted to go but felt if I cancelled everything and hid away then all my stress would somehow disappear. I'd decided to apologise to Miss Taylor also when I went back to work on Monday.

Mrs Dawson handed me my tea which I blew on and took a sip.

'This is the best tea I've ever had,' I said. 'You know how to make it just right.'

It somehow tasted better when someone else made it but perhaps that was just my imagination.

'There's a knack,' replied Mrs Dawson. 'Just

brewed for the right amount of time and a dash of milk. You might like sugar in yours, it might help your nerves.'

'No thanks,' I said, although my nerves were shot but it was more than a spoonful of sugar could sort out.

I felt silly. The slightest thing escalated in my head until I was almost having a panic attack. It happened often but I think that I managed to hide it from most people. Mrs Dawson always knew though.

'I could tell Mr Patel that you're not feeling well,' said Mrs Dawson, 'but say that you might be along later after you've had a lie down.'

I thought about it for a few seconds. It seemed a good idea but what if Mrs Patel had laid on a special meal for me and I didn't turn up? How rude would that appear?

'No,' I said. 'I'll have to just pull myself together and go.'

'Alf used to swear by taking Valerian tablets,' said Mrs Dawson. 'He must have spent a small fortune on them. He got them from that funny little chemist off Portland Place.'

I knew where she meant. It wasn't really a chemist at all. They sold vitamin tablets and holistic medicines for extortionate prices to gullible people who had given up on their doctors. With the likes of Dr McColl, it was no wonder they'd given up.

'Did they work?' I asked.

'Not that I noticed,' she replied, 'but he believed they did so it sort of helped.'

I got up and sat at the kitchen table with Mrs Dawson. My blackbird friend sang loudly - too loudly.

'I've not slept,' I said. 'A few hours sleep and I'll

probably be back to normal. Would you tell Paul that I've been ill and I'll try and still make it?'

It seemed cowardly sending Mrs Dawson to Patel's but that way, if I wasn't better, I could lock the door, close the curtains and hide away.

We drank tea and chatted. Mrs Dawson always managed to have a calming effect on my, allowing me to see things in proportion.

'Is there any more news on the library closure?' she asked.

'We haven't heard anything,' I replied. 'Councillor Evans was meant to be helping things along.'

'I doubt he'll do much,' said Mrs Dawson, unwrapping a new packet of Rich Tea biscuits and offering me one.

It was unusual for Mrs Dawson to eat her biscuits straight from the packet. She usually presented them on a small side plate. I suppose today she felt that there'd been enough stress without fiddling on with side plates. I dunked my Rich Tea into my tea and a bit fell off into the cup. That's all I needed.

'Never mind, dear,' said Mrs Dawson. 'I can get you another one.'

My soaked biscuit floated about in the cup as I tried to rescue it but it eventually fell apart, leaving me with a soggy mess. Mrs Dawson took the cup, poured the tea and the biscuit down the sink and poured me another cup from the teapot.

'I hope it's not stewed,' she said.

'It will be fine,' I replied.

'Alf wanted a front porch,' said Mrs Dawson. 'Councillor Evans was meant to help with that. He never did.'

'Oh,' I said as I drank my tea slowly, avoiding the Rich Tea biscuits that Mrs Dawson had placed in front of me.

'Alf liked writing letters,' said Mrs Dawson. 'Usually ones of complaint, about the bins, planning and such like. He once had a letter from the Queen.'

'Oh,' I said again, not really knowing what to say.

'Well, it wasn't from the Queen,' said Mrs Dawson, 'but from one of her secretaries. Alf had written to congratulate the Queen on her 80th birthday.'

'That was nice of him,' I said.

'She never remembered his birthday,' she joked. I sipped my tea. It was a bit stewed but I said nothing. I didn't want to put Mrs Dawson out.

'We could start a letter writing campaign,' she said. 'To stop the library closure.'

'I'm not sure it would work,' I said. 'And isn't it too late for that?'

I could see that Mrs Dawson had set her mind on the venture and nothing I said was going to stop her.

'I'll start making a list of people we could write to,' said Mrs Dawson. 'Maybe the Prime Minister or whoever deals with public amenities.'

We drank our tea and Mrs Dawson left to visit Mr Patel and to get some shopping. I lay on the couch and as I did so, my bag fell over. The present, neatly wrapped, that Mrs Dawson had given me earlier, fell out. I'd totally forgotten about it and hadn't really thanked her properly for it.

I carefully unwrapped it and smiled. It was a copy of Daphne Du Maurier's Rebecca. I opened the first page. Mrs Dawson had written a message inside which read: 'To my dear friend, Gemma. I hope this book brings

you as much joy as it has me. Fondest regards, Doreen.'
Mrs Dawson had never referred to herself as 'Doreen'
to me before. I folded the floral wrapping paper
carefully to keep and to remind me always of the gift
and placed it on the shelf behind me.
I plumped up the cushions and for the first time read
the words, 'Last night I dreamt I went to Manderley
again'. I was soon totally engrossed in the book.

Chapter Twelve

I awoke at 4pm. I must have dozed off after reading the first chapter of Rebecca. I felt dazed but felt a lot better than I did earlier. I would have to be quick, I only had an hour before I was meant to meet Mr Patel.

I ironed my best dress, jeans and a t shirt seemed just a bit too scruffy. I wondered what Mrs Dawson had told Paul about my day. Had she told him about my argument with Miss Taylor or told him about how she had to bring me home at dinnertime? Or about my migraine or general anxiety? What would he think? With my dress hanging neatly on a hook on the back of the door, I sat down at the kitchen table with a cup of coffee. I remembered what Mrs Dawson told me about the connection between coffee and migraines but I craved a cup and I was sure that one wouldn't do any harm.

From the window, I could see Mr Patel's shop. It all looked very quiet. I could see no activity, no one coming in or out. A small boy rode up and down the street on his bike stopping at the gap between the houses. He dropped his bike on the pavement and disappeared down the narrow lane.

I looked up. There was Norman Drudge, in his window, drinking tea and looking through his binoculars. Further up the street, Mr Bishop was busily polishing his chrome hubcaps. All seemed just how it should be. My blackbird watched and tweeted as I drank my coffee.

I looked up at the clock. It was 4.30pm. I really needed to get ready.

By 4.45pm, I was out of the door and walking briskly to Patel's. I wondered, after Mrs Dawson's visit, if they might not be expecting me at all. I passed Mr Bishop crouched down beside his car.

'Nice evening for it,' he said, as usual, as he continued to polish his Ford Anglia.

I smiled and carried on my way. I realised as I approached the shop that I didn't actually know where the entrance to the Patels' upstairs flat was. There was a door nearby but I thought against knocking on it in case it was the wrong one. Nervously, I entered the shop.

The bell above the door rang twice as I entered. It made me jump slightly.

'Ah, Gemma,' said a smiling Mr Patel Senior, 'we've been expecting you.'

'Hello,' I said uncomfortably.

'How are you feeling now?' he asked. 'Mrs Dawson was in earlier.'

'Much better, thanks,' I replied.

I looked around the shop and saw Sanjay, Paul's

nephew, busily packing the shelves.

'Good,' said Mr Patel Senior. 'Sanjay. Keep an eye on the shop.'

Sanjay smiled up at me, all teeth and sparkling eyes. It was like we were new friends and he wanted to impress me. He took his place behind the counter, barely seeing over the top of it, and focused his eyes on the shop doorway waiting for the next customer.

'We're all upstairs,' said Mr Patel Senior, guiding me towards a curtain that covered the hallway to the shop and led towards bare, uncarpeted wooden stairs. My shoes clunked against them as I proceeded upwards. Wherever the rest of the family were, they must have known that I was on my way. Mr Patel Senior led me to a room, the door was open and there was everyone, Paul, Mrs Patel and three women I hadn't seen before. They were all sat around a wooden table by the window, Mrs Patel was busy filling up the kettle to make a cup of tea. In many ways, it was just like my own front room. I expected it to be, well, more Indian.

'It'll be all rose petals and foreign music,' Mrs Dawson had said earlier.

She'd deduced this after seeing a Bollywood film called Cheetah that had shown at The Odeon.

'I didn't understand any of it,' she complained. 'I thought it would have been more like The King and I.'

Paul saw me and got to his feet. He smiled.

'Gemma,' he said. 'It's lovely to see you. Mrs Dawson said that you were unwell.'

'It was just a migraine,' I said. 'I feel a bit silly taking the afternoon off.'

The three women looked me up and down, not in a

nasty Miss Taylor way, but in a 'we're pleased to meet you' sort of way. I wasn't sure if they could speak English or not so I just muttered a quiet 'hello.' They smiled and nodded.

'Would you like a cup of tea?' asked Paul. 'Please sit down.'

'Yes, I'd love one,' I said as I sat down in the only vacant seat by the table. The women continued watching me, smiling all the time.

'I should introduce you to everyone,' said Paul. 'You know my father, Gupta Patel and this is my mother, Aashna.'

'Pleased to meet you,' I said, even though I'd met Mr Patel Senior in the shop many times before. Mrs Patel smiled at me, a beautiful friendly smile, as she poured the hot water from the kettle into a china teapot and spooned in tea leaves straight from a caddy. I suddenly realised that she was making the tea just as Mrs Dawson would.

'My mother speaks little English,' said Paul. She smiled over again.

'And these three beautiful ladies are my aunties, Brinda and Chandra, and my cousin, Devyani. The boy in the shop is her son, Sanjay.'

'I've met Sanjay,' I said. 'He's a lovely boy.'

'Paul was telling us that you work in the library, Gemma,' said Devyani.

'Yes,' I replied, 'but unfortunately it's closing soon. I don't know what I'll do then.'
Mrs Patel placed seven china cups and saucers on the table and added a dash of milk from a china jug. Devyani leaned forward, closer towards me.

'They're all trying to impress you,' she said smiling. 'Paul is very nervous.'

Devyani was a similar age to me, maybe a bit older, very pretty with, what Mrs Dawson would call, a 'happy face'. Her nose crinkled when she smiled which seemed to be often. I could tell that we were going to get on.

'I hope you like fish and chips?' said Paul.

'Fish and chips?' I inquired.

'Mrs Dawson said that you like fish and chips,' said Paul.

Mrs Dawson and I had once taken a bus trip to Eastbourne where we had sat on the harbour wall eating fish and chips.

'They're lovely,' I'd said, as a rogue seagull tried to steal a chip from my hand. 'I couldn't imagine anything better.'

It had been a perfect day until it suddenly poured down with rain and we had to seek refuge in a seaside shelter.

'I do like fish and chips,' I replied to Paul.

Devyani laughed.

'I think that Gemma was expecting something more Indian,' she said.

Paul gave me a nervous smile.

'I love fish and chips,' I said. 'That will be lovely.'

Paul's aunts were paying particularly close attention to me.

'So, what do you do at the library, dear?' asked Chandra.

It was a simple question but suddenly seemed a very difficult one.

'I check in and out library books,' I replied, 'and file them away.'

I hadn't made myself or my job sound very exciting.

'Oh, that sounds very interesting,' said Brinda.

123

I raised my china cup to my lips. My hand was slightly shaky and my head twitched as the cup met my lips. However, I was sure that no-one had noticed.

'We really must try to do something to keep the library open,' said Mr Patel Senior.

'There's going to be a protest at the Guildhall,' I said. 'Sometime next week, I think.'

'We must all go,' said Brinda. 'Sanjay can run the shop.'

It seemed odd that they would leave an eight year old boy in charge of the shop.

'Oh, he's quite capable,' said Chandra. He won't mind missing school, he can have a cold that day.'

Brinda laughed.

'I wouldn't want to get him into trouble,' I said.

'It will be fine,' said Brinda, tapping the back of my hand, gently, in a friendly sort of way.

'More tea?' she asked, raising the teapot.

'I'm fine, thanks,' I replied.

I could smell the aroma of the fish and chips. Mrs Patel looked slightly flustered at the thought of cooking for seven. When would poor little Sanjay eat, I thought. Perhaps he'd already eaten.

Paul helped his mother place the fish and chips in front of us at the table. Chandra and Brinda looked on as if puzzled by it all. I could tell that they wouldn't normally eat fish and chips. Mrs Patel had even made mushy peas which smelled lovely. Well, to me, anyway.

I looked over to Paul who had taken his place across from me at the table. He looked nervous as did I. We couldn't really talk, well, not in a normal manner. I didn't particularly enjoy eating meals at a table with everyone looking at each other and wondering what to do or say next. I felt comfortable with Mrs Dawson but that was about it. I was never a 'social butterfly' as Mrs Dawson had once described herself in her twenties.

'Eat up,' said Devyani. 'Before it gets cold.'
I nervously cut a piece off the fish and ate it. It had an unusual taste, quite unlike the fish and chips that Mrs Dawson and I had eaten at Eastbourne.

'It's lovely,' I said.
Mrs Patel smiled which seemed to tickle Mr Patel Senior.
To stop myself feeling uncomfortable and jittery, I imagined myself eating fish and chips on the seafront with Mrs Dawson, shooing away hungry seagulls.

'Do you know the man with the binoculars?' asked Devyani. 'He's always sat in his window watching something or other.'
I was surprised that Devyani had spotted him, I thought that it was just something that only Mrs Dawson and me had noticed.

'Oh, that's Norman,' I said. 'Only he's not called Norman, he's called Gerald. Norman is what me and Mrs Dawson call him.'
I felt like I was gibbering, making a fool of myself, so I decided not to explain the situation any further.

'He does look like a Norman,' said Devyani. 'Very serious, very upright.'

'I think that he watches the foxes,' I said. 'There's a mother and cubs in the lane across the way from his house.'

'Oh, we really must have a look,' said Brinda.

'Norman is the man closing the library,' I said, while carefully eating my fish and chips.
I took a sip of tea.

'He's employed by the council,' I said. 'I've seen

him at work several times.'

Paul looked up from his meal. We looked into each other's eyes for several seconds and he half smiled, like a smile that he wanted to make bigger but didn't because he was in company.

'Norman comes in our shop regularly,' said Paul.

It seemed funny Paul calling Gerald Williams 'Norman'.

'He always buys Weetabix,' continued Paul. 'Oh, and a bottle of milk. The little bottles.'

'Does he ever say anything?' I asked.

'Just 'hello' and 'lovely weather,' but nothing else,' replied Paul.

'We really need to talk to this Norman fellow,' said Mr Patel Senior, 'to see if there's any way to keep the library open.'

Mrs Patel looked at him lovingly, not sure what anyone was really saying.

'Perhaps Paul could refuse to sell him Weetabix,' Devyani joked.

I finished my fish and chips. They were certainly different from what I was used to but I wasn't about to be so impolite as to let on.

'That was lovely,' I said.

Devyani, Chandra and Brinda didn't look very convinced.

'Can I help with the washing up?' I asked, standing up slightly holding my plate.

'No, that's fine, dear,' said Chandra. 'Please sit down.'

I could feel my headache coming back and I was keen to leave but I sat down anyway.

'Perhaps we could go for an evening stroll,' said

Paul.

'Yes, that would be lovely,' I replied.
Fresh air and exercise sometimes helped when I felt
stressed. We hadn't really had a chance to talk to each
other at all so it seemed a good idea.

'We could all go and see the foxes,' said
Chandra. 'If they're still there, that is.'
Paul had meant for us to go for a walk on our own, just
me and him, but didn't get a chance to say.

'I would like that very much,' said Brinda.

127

Chapter Thirteen

The entrance to the walkway still had the boy's bike resting at the beginning, discarded as if no-one was ever coming back for it. It was one of those bikes that looked like it may have once belonged to someone else, a hand-me-down, I suppose. Flaking paint on its frame had been rubbed down and re-painted. It was perfectly usable but everyone wanted everything new nowadays.

'They don't know they're born today,' Mrs Dawson would say often. 'We were happy with hand-me-downs and second-hand toys. It's all there was. We were pleased to get anything.'

I didn't think that Paul's family would be interested in the foxes but there we all were waiting to see what we could find. Little Sanjay had left the shop and joined us.

'He has a keen interest in wildlife,' his mother had told me. 'He's such a gentle, little boy.'

Mrs Patel was left running the shop. I'd expected her to put her feet up after cooking tea but she seemed happy to keep the business running. With her little English and bad ankle, I wondered how she was going to cope.

'Have you ever walked down this lane before?' asked Paul, as he eyed up the many weeds growing out of the cracks in the pavement. 'It's very narrow, isn't it? Do you think we're even allowed down here?'
It was odd. I'd walked by the walkway hundreds of times on my way to work but I'd never thought to deviate from my path and explore the small lane. It was almost as if it was a place where I wasn't welcome, or was daunting in some sort of way. It was certainly a lane that no-one seemed to bother much with. Even the council and our own road sweeper avoided it leaving it an overgrown mess.

'I've never been this way before,' I replied, looking at the moss-covered ancient red brick walls on either side of the lane which were covered in graffiti. Someone had sprayed 'EDL - Foreigners Go Home' on one of the walls in blood-red paint. It wasn't at all artistic. It certainly wasn't a Banksy. Mr Patel Senior saw me staring at it. I felt embarrassed, thinking that the Patels would somehow think it was aimed at them. They did live directly opposite, after all.

'I think EDL is an energy company,' said Mr Patel Senior. 'They won't get many customers with that slogan.'
He kept a straight face but I was sure he must have been joking. He was joking, wasn't he?

Already I was having my doubts about proceeding any further. It didn't look at all inviting, I could imagine a gang of skinheads jumping out at any second and attacking us.

'I think it leads to the allotments,' said Mr Patel Senior, realising I was slightly worried. 'Mr Raman has one. He grows carrots and cabbages. It's perfectly safe.'

'Oh,' said Brinda. 'It's a bit dirty looking, isn't it?'

Old crisp packets, remnants of soggy cardboard boxes and other discarded rubbish lay on the floor as well as an abandoned broken up wheelie bin on which someone had written 'Johno is King'.

We stared at the lane apprehensively until little Sanjay pulled on my hand and started leading me down it. Everyone followed. It carried on for about twenty metres, then turned sharp left before it led on to a big expanse of land covered with many small allotments. There was a strange smell, rather like boiled cabbage.

'I didn't know that any of this was here,' I said. 'It's so beautiful.'

It felt as if we had left the city altogether and were now in the open countryside. It reminded me of The Secret Garden, a book that I'd devoured as a child.

'We all play here,' said Sanjay, spotting the boy who had left his bike at the beginning of the lane, sat on a nearby bench.

'Jack,' he shouted. 'Have you seen them?'

Sanjay let go of my hand and ran across to him. The boy looked temporarily surprised but smiled when he recognised his friend. Jack looked a typical boy, well, the sort you used to get, dressed in his old clothes, a bit scruffy looking with shorts and scuffed knees.

Mrs Dawson said that she hadn't seen a 'proper boy' for

130

years.

'We used to have proper boys playing out, constructing go-karts, building dens right up to the 1980s,' she'd said, 'What happened?'

'Today they're all sat at home on their computers,' she'd continued, 'playing games, watching videos or whatever they do nowadays. And if you do see one at all, they've got their head buried in a mobile phone.'

I was sure there were still many 'proper boys', as Mrs Dawson called them, around but just in shorter supply.

'They're over there,' Jack whispered, as he held his camera phone to his chest. 'You'll have to be very quiet.'

We all gathered behind Jack who was now looking slightly agitated that he had so much company. Fox hunting, for him, had been a solitary sport. We stared carefully at the undergrowth as it moved about gently in the breeze. I'm sure that he wasn't happy at all about us all being there.

'Over here,' said Brinda, pointing to a particularly overgrown allotment. We all turned quickly to look that way.

'I think that's a ginger cat,' said Mr Patel Senior before it leapt onto a shed roof happily chasing a blue tit which soon flew off. Old Mr Mainwaring, who worked in the Co-op during the week, had put up an array of feeders on the side of his shed to attract small birds.

'He's an odd little man,' Mrs Dawson had once said. 'Always going on about his King Edward's.'

Mr Mainwaring had two pet rabbits, Gilbert and George, which lived in a hutch in his back yard. I could see them from my back bedroom window. They

131

seemed to be his only company. Mrs Dawson said that Mr Mainwaring had once had a wife but she had left him twenty years previously. Now Gilbert and George were his only friends who he tended to every morning before he went to work and every evening when he returned home. They were treated to fresh carrots, straight from his allotment.

'You can't beat home-grown stuff,' he'd once said to Mrs Dawson after giving her a bag of runner beans.

The sun glinted on the well-polished glass window of Mr Mainwaring's shed. One pane was cracked and broken, probably caused by a stone or football kicked by a 'proper boy'.

'Is that it over there?' asked Chandra, pointing to a scorched brown patch of grass.

Sanjay's friend looked dismayed. He'd been having a quiet day, exploring, watching wild animals and now we'd all turned up and ruined it.

'We won't see them now,' he said. 'It's far too busy and noisy.'

He said the word 'noisy' louder than the rest to make sure that we knew it was our fault that the foxes weren't putting in an appearance.

He didn't seem particularly happy but I suppose we had slightly spoiled his day. He got off the bench, waved goodbye to his friend, and headed off back along the lane to the point where he'd left his bike.

Brinda and Chandra quickly sat down in the vacant spot, wriggling slightly to get comfortable.

'I'm sure that they're making these benches smaller,' said Brinda, as she tried to get settled.

The cheaply constructed bench moved from side to side, its wooden struts in desperate need of replacement. The ornate metal ends had lost most of their green paint and had now turned a dark, rusty colour.

'He goes to my school,' said Sanjay looking up at me. 'He's in my class. He's very good at maths.'
I smiled.

'I'm not very good at maths,' he continued, 'although I try.'
Like Sanjay, I hadn't understood Maths at school. My teacher, Mr Dunstan, had called me a 'nincompoop' in class and said that I would never amount to anything. I'd seen him recently, drinking wine, straight from the bottle, in the nearby precinct. We looked at each other but he didn't seem to recognise me. I wondered if maybe my lack of being able to grasp maths had, somehow, turned him to drink. School hadn't agreed with me, but, it appeared, it hadn't agreed with him either. Hopeless bullying from the other children and the teachers hadn't made school a happy place for me. I loved English, however, spending dinner times in the school library reading whatever I could get my hands on, escaping into mystery stories by Enid Blyton or travelling to Narnia with C S Lewis. Insults from teachers like Mr Dunstan could never take any of that away from me. I doubt that Mr Dunstan had ever even read a book. Well, not a proper one, anyway. Maths books didn't count.

'That's good,' I said to Sanjay. 'All you can do is try your best.'
I realised as I said it that I was sounding very much like Mrs Dawson. She said 'all you can do is try your best' to me often.
Mr Patel Senior leaned closer to me.

'Everything is automated nowadays,' he said.

133

'Children don't need maths so much anymore. Even the till in the shop tells you how much change to give.'

'It was different in my day,' he continued. 'You were beaten with a wooden cane if you didn't know your multiplication tables.'

Mrs Dawson had said something similar. The 'good old days', she called them, only they weren't.

'Oh,' I said. 'That's awful.'

Mr Patel Senior shrugged his shoulders.

'We didn't know any different. That's just how things were back then,' he said. 'It's a different world nowadays. And of course, that was India but I believe it was the same here in England.'

There was a commotion in the distance as the ginger tom shot quickly up onto Mr Mainwaring's shed chasing after a pigeon. Startled, the pigeon managed to escape, flapping its wings desperately, before it landed on another shed close by, cooing loudly as if mocking the cat.

'It's lovely here,' said Chandra. 'We should come here more often. It's amazing that all this is just across the way from the shop.'

Mr Patel Senior watched a skylark twittering about above the long grass in the distance. Other birds chirped away and a lone rook sat perched on a fence post watching an allotment owner digging over his patch. It barely moved as it watched him intently but then suddenly started cawing as loud as it possibly could. Maybe it wanted feeding or perhaps it was trying to attract a mate, either way, it was making an almighty racket.

'It's so peaceful,' Mr Patel Senior said, obviously ignoring the wild sound of the rook. 'You wouldn't think that we were near the main road at all.'

He was right, the walls surrounding the allotments completely cut out much of the noise coming from the passing traffic.

Paul smiled at me, a smile that said he thought, perhaps, I was finding his family a bit overwhelming. It did seem odd being out with so many people, it was just usually me and Mrs Dawson on our regular jaunts to the duck pond. Even so, I felt quite comfortable although I was looking forward to settling down in my flat later, on my own, curled up with a book or watching the television. There was a Stewart Granger film on channel 81 later that evening. Moonfleet was a tale of smuggling and Stewart swashbuckled with the best of them. I'd seen it many times. Mrs Dawson said that her old milkman had had a look of Stewart Granger.

'Supermarkets and cardboard cartons spelled his downfall,' said Mrs Dawson.

'Stewart Granger?' I asked.

'No, dear,' said Mrs Dawson, 'the milkman. I don't know what happened to Stewart Granger.'
Past conversations with Mrs Dawson continued in my head as we sat looking at the allotments. My ability to drift away into another world made me wonder if I might be slightly autistic. I certainly had a routine of checking to see if all the plugs in the house were switched off and pulled out before I left for work but that was normal, wasn't it?

'Better safe than sorry,' Mrs Dawson always said.
Paul's voice suddenly brought me back to the real world.

'Do you fancy a walk around the allotments, Gemma?' he asked.

It still seemed odd to me Paul calling me 'Gemma'. As long as he didn't start calling me 'Gems'. We'd had a 'Gems' at the library for a while on work experience. She was about sixteen, very spotty with wiry wild red hair. I'm sure that she meant well but her loud, constant chattering, got on everyone's nerves, even the normally relaxed, calm Mr Peters.

'That girl could talk for England,' Mrs Dawson had once said on a visit to the library. 'When is she leaving?'
I often wondered what happened to 'Gems' after she left the library. She'd said that she'd wanted to become a reporter but Callum had seen her working behind a desk at the local Job Centre. Callum dreamed of a job at The Final Frontier but none were available. He would sometimes talk to me in Klingon which was most annoying although hilarious to him. Perhaps Gems wasn't so bad, after all.

'Do you fancy a walk?' Paul asked again, realising that no-one had been listening.
Chandra shifted her weight on the bench to get more comfortable.

'Yes, we could all go,' she said, elbowing Brinda. 'This bench is particularly hard. I'm sure that I'll have the pattern of it pressed into me for many days.'
She moved to get up which proved a slightly difficult task with the unsteadiness of the bench and Chandra's shifting weight.

'Let them go on their own,' said Devyani, smiling over to me and knowing that we probably wanted to be on our own.

'Yes, you two go for a walk,' said Brinda. 'We could sit here and watch the sunset.'

Paul and I set off. The allotments covered a huge expanse of land, spreading hundreds of metres into the distance where they met the high walls of the old houses in Duberry Street. The buildings had once housed doctors, solicitors and the like and had been very posh in their time but today were very run down and consisted mostly of bedsits.

'There are a lot of drug users in Duberry Street,' Mrs Dawson had once said. 'Make sure you don't go anywhere near there, dear.'
I wasn't sure how Mrs Dawson knew about the drug habits of the residents of Duberry Street but with its scruffy exterior and general unkempt appearance, I wasn't about to go into one anytime soon, not even to retrieve an overdue library book.

'I can't believe that I didn't know any of this was here,' I said as we carried on our walk.
Paul gazed over towards the many sheds with their trellis fencing, an array of various colours, together with random bamboo poles covered in beans and various climbing plants.

'It sort of reminds me of Mumbai,' said Paul. 'All the allotments on top of each other aren't unlike the slums at Dhravi. Do you know that over a million people live there, crowded in small houses and huts?'
I didn't know. I hadn't heard of Dhravi at all although I'd seen the overcrowded living conditions in India on a BBC Four documentary on a dark winter night when there were no good films on.

'My father would like to return,' said Paul. 'He was born there. My mother likes it too much here though. She never wants to go back.'

'Have you ever been there?' I asked.

'I was also born there,' said Paul, ' but we

travelled to Britain when I was just three years old so I don't remember much about it. Brinda says that it's very hot and also very smelly. There are lots of flies, especially in the summer months.'

I thought that Paul had been born in England. Even with his Indian accent, I hadn't imagined that he had ever lived abroad. I thought that his accent came from his parents. Sanjay had an Indian accent and had never been out of the country as far as I knew.

'Maybe I'll go back one day,' said Paul. 'For a holiday. Perhaps one day, we could go together.'

I liked the sound of that even though Brinda's description of it being hot and smelly didn't sound particularly appealing. I didn't like flies at the best of times, always entering open windows in the summer and landing on everything. I didn't like to kill them so would chase them out of the flat with an old rolled-up tv guide.

I wondered what Mrs Dawson would make of me travelling to India. The closest she'd got to India was watching a DVD of an old television show called 'It Ain't Half Hot, Mum.' The BBC didn't show it anymore, saying that it was racist and offensive.

'Alf wouldn't have liked India,' she'd said. 'Too many bugs, he hated bugs of any sort. And their sewerage system leaves a lot to be desired.'

'India is a very rich country,' continued Paul, 'but it is also a very poor country. Some people live in appalling conditions. However, it's bustling and very vibrant.'

Images of busy and colourful India raced through my mind until the sound of the birds at the allotments, all chattering away at each other, together with the cawing rook, brought me straight back home. I was sure that this was where my blackbird, must live when he wasn't singing on my window ledge.

'I hope my family weren't too overbearing,' said Paul. 'My aunties like to ask lots of questions.'

'They're lovely,' I said. 'I had a great time.'

'If you come again, we'll have to have something more exotic than fish and chips,' Paul joked. 'You will come again, won't you?'

'Of course I will,' I replied. 'That would be lovely.'

We stared over the allotments towards the red sky in the distance. A man was busily piling cut branches and grass on to a bonfire. The smell of the smoke seemed to be everywhere, although it wasn't an unpleasant smell. It reminded me of cosy winter nights in doors reading a book or watching the television. Mrs Dawson had said, at one time, everyone had had a coal fire but they'd long since disappeared.

'I'm sorry about sending Mrs Dawson into the shop,' I said. 'She asks a lot of questions. It's not that she's nosy, she just likes knowing what's what. Perhaps that's the same thing.'

'No one could ask more questions than my aunties,' Paul joked. 'Most customers don't get to leave the shop without revealing something about themselves. Did you know that Mr Graves once had a sausage dog named Stanley?'

I didn't know that. Mr and Mrs Graves didn't seem like doggy sort of people to me. I couldn't really imagine either of them ever walking a tiny Dachshund.

'Mr Graves was heartbroken when it died,' said Paul. 'Although that was thirty three years ago.'

I wondered how Paul's aunties had gleaned this bit of information from Mr Graves, a man who had little to say at the best of times.

'My mother and father have promised to take Mrs Dawson to the bingo,' Paul continued.
I didn't imagine Mr and Mrs Patel playing bingo. I knew Mrs Dawson loved it from our time in Eastbourne. 'Kelly's Eye number 1, two little ducks 22, legs 11.' It was a different world to me. Why didn't they just read the numbers out rather than talking in riddles.

'Alf loved his bingo,' Mrs Dawson had said. 'He had his own dabber. He once won me a lovely fruit bowl and a large stuffed toy lion.'
I'd seen the fruit bowl which took pride of place on Mrs Dawson's dining room table in her front room. Its ornate engraving caught the light as it shone in her house and reflected the pattern on to the nearby table. I think they called it carnival glass, a fact I'd gleaned from watching Fiona Bruce on Antiques Roadshow one Sunday evening.

'I could never get rid of that,' Mrs Dawson had once said while sorting out knick-knacks for the charity shop.

'I know what you're thinking,' said Paul. 'Mrs Patel doesn't understand English but manages to play bingo. My father helps her out although she never wins. It drives him crazy sometimes.'

'Has Brinda and Chandra ever been?' I asked, imagining the whole family, dabbers in hand, desperately waiting for their numbers to be called out, in the hope of winning an unusual ornament or an oversized cuddly toy.

'Only once,' said Paul. 'I think they thought that 'two fat ladies 88' referred to them.'
We both laughed.

In the distance, a small man was busily

investigating the undergrowth. As we got closer, I could see that it was Norman Drudge.

It was warm but he had on a large pair of green rubber Wellingtons. Wellingtons weren't seen in the city much except, perhaps, worn by women who aspired to be middle class who went shopping with small wicker baskets and drove oversized 4x4 Range Rovers. Mrs Graham was such a person. She lived two doors down from Mrs Dawson. Her husband always wore jodhpurs, riding boots, a waistcoat and a flat cap, as if he was about to enter a dressage competition.

'He only works at the Land Registry,' Mrs Dawson said. 'You would think that he was lord of the manor.'

'Hello,' I said to Norman, feeling sure that he would recognise me.

He gave me a quick glance before returning to what he had been previously doing.

'Good evening,' he replied to us both, obviously oblivious to who I was as he looked downwards into the grass. He was fascinated by something.

'I work in the library,' I said, feeling I needed to explain myself. 'We live in the same street.'

'Oh,' he replied, holding out his hand for us to shake it. 'I'm Gerald Williams.'

'I know,' I said. 'Er, we met in the library?'

Paul shook his hand and then I did while saying 'hello' yet again.

'There are a family of dormice here somewhere,' said Norman.

I couldn't imagine ever thinking of Norman as 'Gerald'.

'They're very rare,' he replied. 'You need a licence to handle them.'

We both leaned forward to see if we could see anything

which seemed to unnerve Norman for a second who took a slight step backwards.

'It's a shame about the library,' said Paul. 'Its closing, I mean.'

Norman half-smiled.

'It is a shame,' said Norman. 'I've been working hard to keep it open.'

'Oh,' I said. 'I thought that you were working to close it.'

Norman looked surprised as if I would be aware of all of the ins and outs of the library closure.

'I work for the council,' said Norman, 'and I've got to follow their policies but I've been against the closure since it was first suggested. It's part of the community. We need more community.'

I was suddenly seeing Norman in a different light. He wasn't the uncaring, unfeeling tyrant, recklessly shutting down libraries, that I thought he was. Perhaps, one day, I'd even call him by his real name, Gerald.

'The protest, the television and press coverage have all made the council re-think the idea,' he continued. 'There's a growing feeling that communal areas need to be saved not done away with.'

'So the library won't shut?' I asked.

'It's early days,' he said, 'but I'm hopeful.'

He leaned closer to the clump of grass.

'There, look,' he said. 'There's one of the little fellows.'

Paul and I leaned closer and saw the prettiest little mouse I'd ever seen. It seemed as fascinated with me as I was with it. It held on tightly to the stem of a plant, it's long tail curling over its body to its head.

'It seems so tame,' I said. 'And lovely.'

'Too tame, sometimes,' replied Norman. 'It can

lead to their downfall. There are many cats around
here. Too many, perhaps.'
Norman was right about the amount of cats in the area.
There were at least seven in our street, two of which
Mrs Dawson fed regularly. She called them Little and
Large, due to their size but neither of us knew their real
names or who they belonged to. I liked Little who
would curl up at my feet whenever I visited Mrs
Dawson, but Large was a cantankerous animal who
was a bit overprotective of Mrs Dawson. It clawed and
scratched at me and sometimes stood guard at the front
door, hissing and looking as if it would attack at any
moment. Only Mrs Dawson seemed to be able to calm
it down.
The sun was starting to set and the sky was a beautiful
orange colour.
        'We really should get back,' said Paul. 'It was
lovely meeting you, Mr Williams.'
Norman seemed very happy amongst nature, away
from his front room window.
        'I'll see you in the shop, Mr Patel,' said
Norman.
        'Weetabix?' Paul joked.
        'Of course,' replied Norman before he returned
to his dormouse watching in the fading light.
        'He seems nice,' I said as we walked away.
'Nicer than I thought. It's funny how you can see a
person one way and then see them in a totally different
light once you get to know them.'
I felt guilty for judging Norman before I knew him. I
even felt guilty thinking of him as 'Norman Drudge'
although I wasn't sure how I was going to ever get that
name out of my head.
We got back to the bench but Paul's family had already

left. The seat looked worse for wear. I could see that it might collapse any day now.

'Aunt Chandra wouldn't have been happy missing Coronation Street,' said Paul. 'I'm sure that she thinks it's real.'

In many ways, she was just like Mrs Dawson. She hadn't missed an episode of the show since 1960.

'She laughs at Dev,' said Paul. 'She tells me that an Indian shopkeeper would never behave like that. He seems quite normal to me.'

It was turning chilly and the light was quickly disappearing. Paul took off his jacket and placed it around my shoulders.

'Thanks,' I said, somehow feeling very secure wearing his coat, 'but you'll be cold yourself.'

Paul had a red t-shirt on which had turned an odd shade of pink after many washes. It had the word 'Adidas' embroidered in one corner.

'It's okay, I'm fine, I'll walk you to your door,' replied Paul. 'You can never be too safe.'

As we passed Patel's, I thought that I caught a glimpse of Mrs Patel watching us from the top window. The net curtains moved slightly as if they'd just been caught by a slight breeze. A light was on upstairs but soon went off.

'Are you doing anything tomorrow?' asked Paul.

'Just working in the charity shop in the morning,' I said. 'I'll probably see Mrs Dawson. She likes looking at the knick-knack section.'

'Oh,' said Paul.

'We've got a large collection of vinyl records to sell,' I said. 'Have you got a record player?'

'No,' said Paul. 'But I believe my father has one

144

somewhere. I think that its shoved under the bed. He gets it out occasionally.'

'Does he like easy listening music?' I asked. 'Frank Sinatra, Dean Martin, Shirley Bassey? There are lots of those type of records in the shop.'

'Oddly, he likes country and western,' said Paul. 'It's funny hearing him sing it in an Indian accent. He likes to sing loudly in the shower and we can all hear him. I don't think that he realises. It makes Sanjay laugh very much.'

I didn't like to dwell too long on the image I had in my head of Mr Patel Senior singing into his loofah in the shower while bellowing out Hank Williams.

'His favourite is Johnny Cash,' said Paul. Somehow Mr Patel Senior didn't look much like a Johnny Cash fan.

We got to the three steps leading to my front door. They were cracked and overgrown with moss and quite slippery. I should really get the landlord to look at them, I thought.

'It's been a lovely evening,' said Paul, pointing upwards. 'Look, the stars are out. There's Venus.'

It was hard to see anything amongst the glare of the street lights but I stared skywards anyway. I thought that I could see something but I wasn't sure. I could, however, see a large aeroplane heading back to the airport.

There was an awkward silence.

'Cup of tea?' I asked.

Chapter Fourteen

I got to the charity shop just before 9.30am on Saturday morning. The door creaked loudly as I opened it. Mrs Walters was already there when I arrived.

The shop had an aroma that you didn't find anywhere else. I suppose it was the smell of old clothes; the smell of people's past lives. The library also had its own aroma, the smell of the much-read pages of old books and Mr Thomas. Mr Thomas came in often, mainly to get in out of the rain. Mrs Dawson said that he'd gone 'a bit funny' after his parents had died. I sympathised with him but, even so, he could have done with a good wash.

'Hello, dear,' said Mrs Walters. 'I'll put the kettle on.'

We always had a cup of tea before we started work properly. Early mornings on Saturday were always very quiet but things usually started to get busier at about 11am.

'Had a good week?' asked Mrs Walters as she poured boiling water into our two mugs and dunked a teabag in each.

The mugs came from the charity shop. Mine had a picture of the Spice Girls on it while Mrs Walters had the slogan 'I shot JR?' on hers. I wasn't sure who JR was. Whoever he was, I felt confident that Mrs Walters wouldn't have shot him.

'I've had a lovely week,' I said, although that wasn't entirely true due to my earlier migraine which had now miraculously cleared up. Walking with Paul at the allotments had lifted my mood greatly. I felt far more positive about life in general.

'We had a very peculiar man in here on Tuesday,' said Mrs Walters as she sipped her tea. 'He was looking for used underpants. What sort of person buys second-hand underpants?'

I didn't know what the correct answer was.

'That's odd,' I said imagining a man desperately rummaging through a bin liner for someone else's under garments.

I blew on my tea and took a sip. It tasted far better than the library's cheap tea.

'How are things at work?' Mrs Walters asked, changing the subject.

'I had an argument with Miss Taylor,' I said. Mrs Walters knew exactly who Miss Taylor was and had seen her on many occasions while visiting the library. Mrs Walters liked romantic fiction particularly Mills and Boon. There were plenty of books in the

147

charity shop but for some reason, she always came into the library on a Wednesday afternoon.

'It'll be for the company,' Mrs Dawson had once said.

'Oh, Miss Taylor,' said Mrs Walters. 'I can imagine that she's very difficult. Best to take no notice of her. Those sort of people don't like being ignored.' She ran a cloth along the top of the counter clearing it of dust. Speckles of the dust gathered in the rays of the sunlight shining through the front window. They hung in the air until a rogue cloud blocked the sun's path.

'The shop really needs a proper clean,' said Mrs Walters. 'Perhaps we should get those two women off the telly in.'

I think that she meant Aggie and Kim who appeared on How Clean is Your House, a programme I'd stumbled on one rainy afternoon, repeated on some obscure Freeview channel that only a handful of people probably watched. Cockroaches, bugs and cats' mess seemed to be the main problems. The charity shop had none of those and was actually quite tidy in comparison. Who minded a bit of dust, after all?

'There's a chance that the library might be saved,' I said. 'I was talking to a man from the council. He lives near me. You know, the one I told you about who's always sat in his window, looking through binoculars and drinking tea and eating biscuits.'

'Norman?' she asked.

'Yes,' I replied. I was surprised that she referred to him as Norman although I mentioned his antics every time I was in the charity shop. Mrs Walters usual reply was 'how strange' although I suppose everybody drank tea and ate biscuits at some point.

'The protests and media coverage seem to have

helped,' I said. 'There was a picture of the staff in the Chronicle.'

'Well, that's good,' replied Mrs Walters. 'Fingers crossed.'

Mrs Walters crossed her fingers for most things in her life. I wasn't sure if it helped or not but she did seem quite lucky. She'd once won a holiday to Egypt in a PG Tips competition.

'Dirty, smelly place,' she said at the time. 'I wouldn't want to go again. Everybody's after your money.'

Mrs Walters rested her mug on the counter and got up.

'Look what came in earlier,' she said, taking a small square box off the nearby shelf. 'I've been dying to show it to you all week.'

She placed the box on the table. It was white with an embossed floral pattern on the side. It looked almost new as if it had never been unpacked.

'Go on, open it,' she said.

I gently lifted the lid off the box. There inside was a wine glass, a china mouse and a Siamese cat.

'Mrs Dawson has been looking for one of these for ages,' I said, excited, glad that one had finally been discovered.

'I know,' replied Mrs Walters. 'I don't think it's ever been taken out of the box.'

'She will be pleased,' I said. 'I wonder if I should wrap it up for her? So it's more of a surprise.'

I took it out and stood the glass up, placed the mouse inside and rested the Siamese cat on the edge of the glass looking in.

'It's quite unusual,' I said. 'I don't think I've ever seen one before.'

'They were all the rage at one time,' said Mrs

Walters. 'It reminds me of our Karen.'
Mrs Walters paused for a few seconds, no doubt
thinking about her sister. I thought that she might cry
but then she fought against it and smiled.

'Oh, well,' she said. 'Times change, I suppose.'
She produced some wrapping paper, a pale yellow
colour with white stripes. It had been donated after a
card shop in the precinct had closed down. We had also
been given a lot of Christmas cards but no-one was
interested in them much as summer approached so they
lay in the back store room waiting until the seasons
changed.

'We could wrap it in this,' said Mrs Walters,
slowly pulling the wrapping paper off its cardboard
tube. 'It's very pretty, isn't it?'
In that moment, I realised how lucky I was to have
friends like Mrs Walters and Mrs Dawson. We were
friends, Mrs Walters and I, even though we only saw
each other on Saturdays in the charity shop and
occasionally in the library. We weren't as close as Mrs
Dawson and I but even so we seemed to knock along
pretty well.

For the next ten minutes, we wrapped up Mrs
Dawson's present, carefully sellotaping it before Mrs
Walters stuck on a nice pink bow in the corner.

'It looks lovely,' I said. 'I'll put some money in
the box. Do you think five pounds would be enough?'

'I'm sure that's fine, dear,' she said, smiling at
the now beautifully wrapped up gift.
Anything we weren't sure of the price of, Mrs Walters
always put out for £4.99.

'They think they're getting it cheaper,' she said,
'if it's got 99p on the end. Everyone's looking for a
bargain.'

She was right, of course, and most stuff seemed to disappear within a few days.

The buzzer above the door let out a loud 'brrr' noise so we left what we were doing and went out into the main part of the shop. There was Mrs Dawson.

'Hello Gemma, hello Mrs Walters,' she said. 'It's a lovely day.'

Her gaze averted from us for a couple of seconds as she looked briskly around the shop, desperate to see what was new.

I was always glad to see Mrs Dawson but perhaps, today, I smiled too much. She could tell I was happy about something.

'I'm just going to sort out the new stock in the backroom,' said Mrs Walters before winking at me and leaving. Mrs Dawson watched her carefully.

'What's she winking for?' Mrs Dawson asked as she placed her shopping bags down on the floor.

'It's a surprise,' I replied.

Mrs Dawson angled her head and body to see if she could get a clearer view of Mrs Walters in the storeroom. She couldn't.

'Oh,' said Mrs Dawson. 'A nice one, I hope.'

'Oh, yes,' I replied.

Before I could say any more, Mrs Dawson had changed the subject.

'How did you get on at the Patels yesterday evening?' she asked.

'They were lovely,' I replied. 'We had fish and chips.'

Mrs Dawson looked surprised.

'Fish and chips?' she said. 'That's not very Indian, is it?'

She glanced quickly around the shop and over to the

knick-knack section to see what new stock there was. Someone had donated a collection of weird, highly coloured glass animals which seemed to take her eye.

'I met Paul's whole family,' I said. 'His aunties, his sister and his parents.'

'That won't have helped your migraine much,' said Mrs Dawson, always concerned about my well-being.

'Oh, and I met Paul's nephew, Sanjay,' I continued.

Mrs Dawson picked up the overfull jar of old pens on the counter and rattled it slightly so they all fell into place before putting it back on to the counter.

'Oh, yes, little Sanjay. I've seen him in the shop,' replied Mrs Dawson. 'He's a lovely boy. He's always very helpful and polite. He has very bright eyes and a big smile, hasn't he?'

'Yes,' I replied. 'And after tea, we all went to the allotments to look for the foxes. I had no idea they were even there, the allotments that is.'

'I believe Mr Raman has one, said Mrs Dawson. 'He's a good friend of Mr Patel Senior.'

'Does he like bingo?' I joked.

'No, I don't think he'd be a bingo type of man,' said Mrs Dawson. 'He's more into carrots and suchlike. I believe he's a widower. I don't like to ask.'

She picked up a leaflet on the counter and started reading it. She squinted slightly and held it at arms length unable to see it properly because her reading glasses were in her handbag.

'I really must get a pair of those glasses you wear around your neck,' she said. 'You know, the ones on a piece of string or a chain. I'd always know where they were then, they'd always be handy.'

'That's a good idea,' I said, imagining Mrs Dawson looking like some crime solving pensioner from one of Agatha Christie's Miss Marple books.

'Only,' she continued. 'They're a bit pretentious, don't you think so, dear? And, anyway, they'd make me feel, well, old.'

'They'd be handy,' I said, not wanting to comment on Mrs Dawson's age. 'You'd always be able to locate them.

Mrs Dawson thought about it for a couple of seconds.

'There's a jumble sale on at the old church hall on Tuesday,' said Mrs Dawson, continuing to read the leaflet. 'Shall we go?'

The last time we'd gone to a jumble sale was at the community hall when we queued for forty minutes to get in. It was mainly rubbish and a fight broke out over a worn brown woolly jumper and a collection of cutlery.

Mrs Dawson was obviously thinking about the event at the same time as I was.

'Perhaps not,' she said. 'I suppose there's more than enough stuff in the charity shop to keep me going.'

'Have you tried ebay?' I suggested. 'It's very popular.'

'Oh, no, dear,' replied Mrs Dawson. 'I couldn't be bothering with the internet. Alice's Rodney has it. He's never off the thing.'

Rodney was Alice's son. Mrs Dawson said that he existed but I'd never actually seen him. He was one of those creatures who never ventured out in the day time, or night time for that matter.

'He's got a girlfriend now,' said Mrs Dawson. 'Rodney, that is. He met her on the internet, by coincidence. She's forty-five. It doesn't seem right, a nineteen year old having a forty-five year old girlfriend, does it, dear?'

'How odd,' I said, which was something I always said whenever I was lost for words.

'They play games and stuff,' Mrs Dawson continued. 'Little beeping men, jumping on and off platforms. Where's the fun in that? Of course, he's never met her. I think she's Bulgarian or Romanian or something similar. One of those countries, anyway.' She placed the leaflet neatly back on the counter, tidily arranging the pile of adverts beneath it.

'I didn't know that you knew Mr and Mrs Patel,' I said. 'You never mentioned it.'

'It's only a recent thing,' said Mrs Dawson. 'We've become friends since I've started going in the shop more.'

'Asking questions about Paul?' I joked.

'Yes, I suppose so,' replied Mrs Dawson, smiling. 'Although they seem to have a good collection of broken biscuits recently.'
Her eyes wandered from me back to the storeroom to see if she could tell what Mrs Walters was up to.

'Something else happened,' I said. 'At the allotments.'

'Oh, yes?' replied Mrs Dawson suddenly curious as to what I was about to tell her.

'We bumped into Norman Drudge,' I said. 'He was looking for dormice.'

'Oh, how strange,' replied Mrs Dawson. 'Did he find any?'

'Oh, yes,' I replied. 'They're lovely creatures. Tiny pink noses and big curly tails.'

'I can't say that I've ever seen one,' said Mrs Dawson. 'We had mice in our old house. Of course, Alf

154

soon made short shrift of them being a rat catcher.'

'How sad,' I said. 'I could never hurt one.'

'They can be very annoying, dear,' said Mrs Dawson. 'Running about at all hours and getting into your cupboards. They're alright in their place, outdoors, that is. Even then, they can be a pest.'

'Oh,' I said. 'They are pretty, though, aren't they?'

Mrs Dawson's face made it clear that she had no time for rodents or other furry vermin.

'I suppose so, dear,' she said. 'Did Norman have anything to say?'

'Oh, yes,' I said. 'He said that there was a chance that the library might not close after all.'

'Well, that is good news, isn't it?' said Mrs Dawson, 'But wasn't he the person trying to shut it?'

I shrugged my shoulders and pulled that face people do when they're not sure of the answer.

'He seemed a very nice man,' I said. 'I think maybe we've got him all wrong. I don't feel right calling him Norman Drudge any more.'

'He does look like a Norman though, doesn't he?' Mrs Dawson joked.

Mrs Walters returned to the shop carrying a mug of tea for Mrs Dawson.

'I thought if you were staying you might like a brew,' she said.

Mrs Dawson eyed up the 'I shot JR' mug. She ran her finger down the side of it.

'That's lovely, thank you,' she said as she moved the mug around to get a clearer view of its slogan.

She pointed to the mug.

'He used to be in I Dream of Jeannie,' she said.

'Who?' I asked.

'JR,' she replied. 'Him off Dallas. You know, the sly older brother. The one who was always trying to get one over on Bobby.'

I'd seen Dallas listed on one of the Freeview channels but had never watched it.

'He was so handsome in I Dream of Jeannie,' she said. 'Always smartly dressed in a uniform. He was an astronaut, I think.'

'Oh,' I said.

'It was very funny,' continued Mrs Dawson. 'He found a genie in a bottle on a desert island. By coincidence, she was called Jeannie. She was very pretty. Now, what was her real name? Barbara, something, I think.'

'I'll have to watch it,' I said.

'I don't think it's on any more, dear,' she replied. 'I don't know what happened to him in later years.'

'Who?' I asked.

'JR,' replied Mrs Dawson. 'Well, Larry Hagman. He seemed to go downhill. Drink, I suppose.'

'Oh,' I said.

'Alf had a look of Larry Hagman,' Mrs Dawson continued. 'The young one, of course, not the old one.' She looked at the mug again and smiled.

'So how did you get on with Paul, away from his family, that is?' asked Mrs Dawson. It was a question she'd been dying to ask since she'd come in the shop.

'Lovely,' I replied. 'After we talked to Norman, we walked around the allotments until the sun set and then he walked me home.'

'Did you ask him in?' Mrs Dawson asked.

'I made him a cup of tea,' I replied. 'He said that it was the best cup of tea he'd ever had.'

'Oh,' said Mrs Dawson, wanting to know what happened next but saying no more because she didn't want to appear to be rude.

'I hope that you didn't use those cheap teabags from Patel's,' she said.

'And then he went home,' I continued. 'We're going to the pictures tonight. Paul wants to see Jurassic World.'

'That's an odd film to take a girl to,' said Mrs Dawson. 'Too many dinosaurs for my liking.'

'I didn't like to say that I'd rather see something else,' I said. 'I'm sure that I'll enjoy it.'
Mrs Walters winked and smiled at me and I nodded back to her.

'Is something going on?' asked Mrs Dawson.

'We've a surprise for you,' I said. 'A present.'
Mrs Walters gently placed the parcel on the table in front of us.

'Oh my,' said Mrs Dawson, scrutinising the package. 'What a lovely wrapped package?'

'It's something that you've wanted for a long time,' I said. 'Go on, open it.'
Mrs Dawson gently pulled at the paper.

'It's very well wrapped up,' she said. 'Whatever is it?'
She removed the bow carefully and put it to one side to use again. Mrs Walters and I watched as Mrs Dawson unwrapped her present.

'It's a box,' she said. 'A rather lovely box.'

'It's what's inside the box,' said Mrs Walters. 'Something special.'
Mrs Dawson gingerly lifted the lid off the top of the

box. She reached inside and pulled out the wine glass, mouse and Siamese cat and placed it on the table. She looked at it intently and looked very happy but then shed a tear which she quickly wiped away with a handkerchief taken from her handbag.

'It's lovely,' she said. 'It really is very lovely. Thank you both, very much.'

She dabbed the corner of her eyes and looked up at me and smiled.

'It's wonderful, thank you,' she said. 'You're a true friend.'

She looked at it once more before carefully packing everything back into it's box.

'I wouldn't want to break such a lovely present,' she said.

It was an uneventful morning in the charity shop after Mrs Dawson left. It was very quiet, no stragglers returning home from Saturday morning shopping.

'There must be tennis or something on the television,' Mrs Walters said. 'That usually keeps them in.'

Neither of us watched the tennis. Mrs Dawson said that it wasn't the same since Björn Borg and John McEnroe had stopped playing.

'McEnroe was always having wild arguments,' Mrs Dawson had once said. 'That was the only reason Alf and I watched it. Chris Evert was very pretty, it kept us entertained the whole summer.'

Mrs Walters managed to sell several of the vinyl records to a man who came in at about 11am.

'I'm looking for Mantovani,' he said as he browsed through the collection.

'I'll have to get Mrs Walters,' I said. 'I'm not sure he works here.'

I don't think the man realised I was joking but seemed to brighten up when Mrs Walters found what he was looking for.

I finished my shift at the shop at 1pm and walked along the tree-lined roads back to my flat. I glanced over at Patel's but couldn't see anything going on. I should have popped in but I didn't want to tie up too much of Paul's time. Anyway, I'd soon be seeing him that evening before we made our way to the cinema.

Mrs Dawson was waiting for me on the front steps when I got back. I felt that I really should give her a spare key. She'd given me hers 'for emergencies' but I'd never used it.

I smiled. I was always glad to see Mrs Dawson. She sort of looked worried about something.

'I hope you haven't been waiting too long,' I said. 'I strolled rather than doing my quick walk.'

'That will be love,' Mrs Dawson joked. 'It does funny things to people.'

'Well, I do suddenly feel very happy,' I said as I fumbled in my bag for the door key.

'I've quite enjoyed just watching the world go by,' said Mrs Dawson. 'I'm surprised Mr Bishop has any paint left on that car the way he polishes it.'

As we looked over to Mr Bishop, he smiled and waved across at us.

'There's something I want to ask you,' said Mrs Dawson. 'I'll tell you when we get in.'

She looked quickly around almost to check to see if someone might be listening. There was no-one in sight, apart from Mr Bishop, of course.

We sat at the kitchen table, drinking tea from our china cups. I wondered what Mrs Dawson had been so desperate to tell me on the front steps.

'You do make a lovely cup of tea,' she said. 'It's really the best I have had all week.'

My friendly blackbird looked in through the window and pecked twice on the glass.

'That's my Alf,' joked Mrs Dawson, 'reincarnated as a bird.'

We smiled.

'Was there something you wanted to tell me?' I asked.

Mrs Dawson took a sip of tea before placing the cup back into its saucer.

'I must thank you again for the present,' she said. 'It looks wonderful on the mantelpiece. You must come around and see it.'

'I will,' I said.

'Oh, and Mr Raman, Mr Patel Senior's friend, has asked me out for dinner,' said Mrs Dawson. 'I hope you don't mind.'

'Why should I mind?' I said. 'I think that's lovely.'

'It's just that with you stepping out with Paul,' she said. 'I thought that you might think that it would somehow complicate things.'

Mrs Dawson always said 'stepping out' which made me smile. She had lots of phrases that she still used which were last heard of in the 1950s.

'Mr Raman is Mr Patel's cousin, apparently,' Mrs Dawson continued.

'I think it's wonderful,' I said. 'We could end up related.'

'I hadn't thought of that,' said Mrs Dawson as she sipped her tea.

'The more I think about it,' she said, 'the more I wonder if I should go.'

'Why not?' I said. 'It will be good to get out and go to a nice restaurant for a change.'

'Only,' started Mrs Dawson.

'Yes?' I replied.

'Only, it doesn't seem long since Alf passed away,' she said. 'And seeing the ornament, sitting there on the mantelpiece, brought back so many happy memories of our time together. Should I really be stepping out with another man?'

'I'm sure Alf would want you to be happy,' I said.

With me saying that, the blackbird tapped twice on the window and looked at Mrs Dawson as if waiting for a reply.

'There,' I said. 'It's decided.'

We sipped our tea and watched as the blackbird walked up and down the window ledge.

'I see that Norman is back in his window,' I said.

'Oh, yes,' replied Mrs Dawson. 'He appears to be reading a copy of The Mail.'

'And drinking tea,' I said.

'From a builder's mug,' continued Mrs Dawson. With that, he saw us and waved over. We both politely waved back. The movement of our hands scared the blackbird and he quickly flew off.

'Oh, how embarrassing,' said Mrs Dawson. 'He's seen us watching him.'

'He's never waved before,' I said.

'Perhaps we could move the table back a bit,' said Mrs Dawson. 'Further away from the window.'

'But wouldn't that appear rude?' I asked. 'And anyway, I like looking out of the window. We just won't look his way.'

Unconsciously, our eyes were drawn back to Norman's window.

'It's definitely The Mail,' said Mrs Dawson. We stared out on to the street. The small boy, Jack, cycled by, riding on the pavement heading towards the allotments.

'He'll knock someone over like that,' said Mrs Dawson.

We watched Mr Bishop pick up his empty bucket to return indoors to get more water.

'Just as well it isn't 1976,' said Mrs Dawson. 'He would have had to have left it dirty.'

I took a final sip of tea, put my cup carefully back in its saucer before placing it in the sink to wash later.

'I've got to apologise to Miss Taylor on Monday,' I said.

'I shouldn't let it bother you, dear,' said Mrs Dawson.

'But it's always in the back of my mind,' I said.

'Well, just don't apologise to her,' said Mrs Dawson, 'and forget all about it.'

'But I've got to say sorry,' I continued, 'it's nibbling away at me. And I made her cry.'

'She's only got herself to blame for that,' said Mrs Dawson.

I stared back out on to the street. There was no sign of Mr Bishop.

'It was Miss Taylor who gave you that migraine in the first place,' said Mrs Dawson. 'If anyone should be apologising, it should be her.'

'I can't help it,' I said. 'I've got to apologise.'

'Oh, well,' said Mrs Dawson as she unwrapped a brand new packet of biscuits for us both.

162

'I've got biscuits,' I said.

'I fancied a custard cream,' said Mrs Dawson. 'Alf loved them. Patel's were selling broken ones but they're not the same, dear, are they?"
She sighed.

'What would Alf have made of this Mr Raman business?' she said. 'Of course, it was frowned upon in my day.'

'What was?' I asked.

'Mixed relationships,' replied Mrs Dawson. 'My mother's friend married an American GI just after the war. She went to live with him in Delaware. He was black, her family never spoke to her again.'

'Oh,' I said. 'But it's 2018, nobody will even take any notice.'

'You'd be amazed how funny people can be,' said Mrs Dawson. 'How they gossip about such things.'

'Just ignore it,' I said. 'Anyway, no-one's saying anything.'

'Mrs Granger gave me a funny look the other day,' said Mrs Dawson.

'Mrs Granger gives everyone a funny look,' I said. 'Anyway, you don't mind me going out with Paul. He's Indian.'

'Yes, but it's different for you,' replied Mrs Dawson. 'You're young.'
I couldn't really see what she was getting at.

'Young people are different nowadays,' she said. 'There's more freedom. It was a different world when I was your age.'

'But Mr Raman's lovely,' I said. 'And you get on well.'

'I know, dear,' replied Mrs Dawson. 'I suppose I'm just being foolish. And, anyway, who cares what the likes of Mrs Granger are saying.'

We both stared out towards the street. Mr Bishop didn't reappear.

'He must be having a cup of tea,' I suggested, looking at his gleaming car standing at the end of the street.

'What time are you going to the pictures?' asked Mrs Dawson.

'Half past seven,' I replied. 'You can come along, if you like.'

'Oh, no, that wouldn't do,' said Mrs Dawson. 'I'm sure that Paul wouldn't want me tagging along. And dinosaurs really aren't my thing anyway.'

'But I'd like you to come,' I said.

'Maybe another time,' said Mrs Dawson, 'when you know each other a bit better, perhaps.'

'He's picking me up from here,' I said, 'and then we're catching the bus.'

'That will be an experience,' said Mrs Dawson. 'You get some very odd people on the bus.'

We were both watching Norman, covertly out of the corners of our eyes. He suddenly got up and disappeared.

'Pretend you're not looking,' said Mrs Dawson.

'I'm not looking,' I said but, of course, I was.

'I hope he can save the library,' I continued.

'So do I, dear,' replied Mrs Dawson.

'Which restaurant is Mr Raman taking you to?' I asked.

'It's a surprise,' replied Mrs Dawson. 'Somewhere in town, I suppose. I'm still not sure it's the right thing to do.'

'Maybe you'll have fish and chips,' I joked.

'I'd be happier eating fish and chips on the sea

164

front somewhere,' said Mrs Dawson. 'I'm not one for swanky restaurants.'

'You should tell him,' I said.

'Oh no, I couldn't do that,' said Mrs Dawson. 'He'll have booked it and everything.'

'When are you going?' I asked.

'This evening,' replied Mrs Dawson.

'Oh,' I replied, not realising that her date was so soon. 'We might see you.'

'It's funny, now you've mentioned fish and chips, I quite fancy some.' said Mrs Dawson. 'Should I nip down to the shop and get some? You haven't eaten, have you?'

'That would be lovely,' I said. 'But I'll come with you and we can eat them in the park. I'm sure the ducks would like the odd chip.'

I got my coat and we set off for Harry Wong's. Harry made the best fish and chips in the area although he didn't speak a word of English. His daughter, May, took most of the orders.

'She's a pretty girl, isn't she?' Mrs Dawson said ten minutes later as we stood in the queue at Harry Wong's waiting to place our order.

Chapter Fifteen

Sunday morning's were usually quiet but I was woken up at 4am, again by someone letting off fireworks. The loud bangs shook the flat, shaking the unwashed dishes that lay in the sink. I looked out of the kitchen window and down the street. The explosions seemed to be coming from down the lane where the allotments were. I craned my neck to get a better view. As I watched a small boy ran out. It was Sanjay. I watched him scuttle back to Patel's, letting himself in at the rear door, closing it quietly so that he could slip in undetected.

It was no good. I'd never get back to sleep now so I

picked up the copy of Rebecca that Mrs Dawson had bought for me. I stared down at its wonderful cover which had a creepy feel to it and showed a desolate home, looking something like a haunted house, with a twisted gnarled tree beside it. I opened the book and began to read. It started with the words, 'Last night I dreamt I went to Manderley again.' Before long, I felt myself totally immersed in the book. I could see why Mrs Dawson loved Daphne Du Maurier so much. I carried on reading, the room turning from darkness to light as the sun slowly came up, until just after 7am. I glanced across at the clock, ticking away loudly in the kitchen. It was too late to return to bed.

I placed the book on the table beside me before wandering over to the kitchen window and pulling over the curtains. My blackbird friend stared back in at me, craning his neck, as if looking to see if I had anything to eat. I took a slice of bread out of the bread bin before breaking it up, opening the window, and scattering it across the window ledge. He chirped in appreciation and started pecking away. Before long, he was joined by two straggly-looking sparrows who were also regular visitors. Mrs Dawson told me that they were house sparrows as opposed to tree sparrows but how she knew the difference I was uncertain.

I wondered how Mrs Dawson's dinner date had gone with Mr Raman? For a moment, I imagined them as Laurence Olivier and Joan Fontaine in the movie version of Rebecca. Was she to become the next Mrs De Winter and be plagued by the constant bullying of Mrs Danvers? Perhaps not.

I thought about my movie date with Paul. Two hours at the cinema seemed to go on forever. Like the library, the cinema had its own smell which was a combination of packaged treats, well-worn seats and a strange detergent smell which the cinema's equivalent to Mrs Dyson had used to clean the theatre after everyone had gone home. The screen was huge, bigger than I'd ever seen, and curved slightly at the edges. The sound boomed with every special effect and its accompanying noise shook the cinema.

I'm sure that I must have fidgeted a lot. I'd got out of the habit of being surrounded by so many people and felt uncomfortable for most of the film. It was also hard to follow with people's mobile phones constantly going off, the rustle of cellophane covered treats and the continued coughing of various people in the audience. I wasn't really into special effects films and hadn't paid much attention to most of it anyway, too nervous to take it all in. It seemed to feature a lot of large dinosaurs, roaring loudly, chasing the same group of people around and around throughout. I couldn't imagine any of the old stars featuring in such films. I couldn't recall a movie with James Stewart or Cary Grant ever being chased by an oversized reptile. But, then I remembered, one of my heroes, James Mason, starring in Journey to the Centre of the Earth. I'm sure that that featured a dinosaur although, perhaps, a bit more papier-mâché than the more modern ones.

I'm sure it was probably good, I just lacked the concentration to enjoy it. Paul bought me an ice cream and a box of Maltesers, which he said were on special offer at the shop. Only 89p apparently. The corner of the box was slightly bashed but that didn't matter. Afterwards, we caught the bus back home. Emo was on the same journey shouting 'tickets, please' to anyone who would listen. His grey, zip-up flying suit looked as if it could do with a good clean. It looked as if someone had rolled him down a hill and into a bog. Perhaps he'd had a fight. There was a strange, unpleasant smell about him today and passengers moved to seats further away once he'd sat down. I felt sorry for him, he seemed to have no-one and I worried about him all the way home, glancing occasionally over my shoulder to see if he was alright. He smiled at one point, it was a wide-eyed crazy sort of smile. He wiggled his fingers in a strange sort of wave. It unnerved me and I didn't turn around again until we got off the bus.

Paul walked me straight to my door. I knew that Emo was harmless but I somehow wouldn't have felt comfortable walking back on my own. As far as I knew, anyway, Emo had stayed on the bus, probably travelling all the way back to the bus station where, I was told, he slept on one of the old rickety wooden benches there. He was in good company. Several local 'tramps' spent the night there, drinking away their worries with cheap bottles of wine from the nearby off-licence which seemed to stay open all night.

Paul and I talked for a bit, just about daft things, before he left and returned to the shop. I quickly found my key and went inside, making sure that the strong wooden door was securely shut behind me. As I made my way up the stairs to my flat, I wondered if Mrs Dawson's date had been more eventful.

I didn't have to wait long to find out. Mrs Dawson called around just after 9am. She always gave two quick, sharp pushes on the bell so from the sound I knew it was her. She worried that I might unwittingly open the door to some unpleasant character. Alan Cole's name was mentioned more than once.

'Put the kettle on, dear,' she said as she sat down at the table by the kitchen window. She looked a bit flustered. She placed her handbag down by her feet.

'I'm too old for this,' she said.

'Too old for what?' I asked. 'Cups of tea?'

'Too old to go on dates with strange men,' she answered.

'Me too,' I joked.

I filled the kettle and plugged it in, turning the spout away from the window so that the steam didn't mist it up. I didn't want to miss anything that might go on out on the street, not that much ever changed.

'Did it not go well?' I asked, sitting down opposite Mrs Dawson at the kitchen table.

'Oh, no, everything was fine,' said Mrs Dawson, wiggling slightly to get comfortable on the thin wooden chair. 'Mr Raman was the perfect gentleman.'

'Oh,' I said, fiddling with a tea cup coaster. I'd bought a set of six from the charity shop. They featured various African birds, none of which I'd heard of. I think that one was some sort of parrot. From the faded drawings on them, it was difficult to tell.

'But he's not Alf,' continued Mrs Dawson, 'and never will be.'

She stared out towards the street glancing over at the kettle which was starting to shake as it partly boiled before switching itself off. Perhaps I should have put less water in it. Hot water poured from its spout onto the side. I got a dish cloth and quickly mopped it up before turning the kettle on once more. It was a routine I went through daily.

'Will you see him again?' I asked.

'I don't know,' said Mrs Dawson. 'It's not Mr Raman's fault but when you've loved someone, really loved someone, it's very difficult to just switch off and find romance with someone else. You'll discover that one day, dear.'

'Oh,' I said. 'Maybe things will change the more you get to know him.'

'Maybe,' said Mrs Dawson.

I could see Mr Granger walking anxiously up and down the street. I saw him haughtily pick up his recycling bag which had blown off down towards Mr Bishop's house. Mr Granger had written his house number on it in dark black felt tip pen together with the words 'Do not remove.' He was very precious about his recycling bag and had accused several neighbours of stealing it in the past.

'Anyway, dear, enough about me,' continued Mrs Dawson. 'How did you get on with Paul at the cinema?'

I looked over towards the unwashed dishes in the sink.

'I had one of my headaches,' I said. 'It's the stress, I suppose.'

'Oh dear,' said Mrs Dawson. 'I don't suppose all those dinosaurs making a racket helped either.'

The kettle finally boiled properly, there was steam everywhere. Water droplets formed on the kitchen tiles. Mould had grown on the grouting due to the daily repeated process. I'd meant to bleach it all but had never got around to it.

'It's supposed to turn itself off. I suppose I should really use the new one,' I said. 'But I don't like to throw anything away. It seems a waste, it works after all.'

The kettle didn't match the rest of the kitchen, it was an odd brown colour, but I wasn't really bothered. Mrs Dawson had bought me a nice red one for Christmas but it remained in its box at the back of the wardrobe. I

171

wanted to get my money's worth out of this one first. Mrs Dawson smiled.

'That's the war time spirit,' she said. 'Make do and mend.'

I poured some warm water into the teapot, swirled it around, emptied it and then added two spoonfuls of tea before adding more hot water.

'Was the film any good?' asked Mrs Dawson.

'I don't know,' I said. 'I prefer the old ones. I was trying to think of movies that featured dinosaurs. Can you think of any? Old movies, that is.'

Mrs Dawson thought about it for a couple of seconds.

'There was that one with Raquel Welch,' she said. 'She was very popular with the men at one time. Rather like her at number ten. You know, the one with the big chest. I think Raquel Welch's son married Fred Truman's daughter.'

'Fred Truman?' I asked.

'He was an old cricket player from Yorkshire, dear,' said Mrs Dawson. 'He appeared in a quiz show featuring bar billiards. I forget what it was called.'

'Oh,' I said. 'What was the film called?'

'I think it was 100 Million Years BC,' said Mrs Dawson. 'Or was it 10,000 Years BC? Something like that. When were dinosaurs around? Raquel Welch wore a bearskin and eye make-up throughout. I think her and her caveman boyfriend fought off a giant lizard or was that Lost World?'

'I'll have to keep a look out for it,' I said, wondering if it might pop up on channel 81 or the Horror channel.

'I wouldn't bother,' replied Mrs Dawson. 'It wasn't very good.'

I rubbed the kitchen tiles over with the cloth that I kept

172

beside the sink specifically for the purpose before wringing it out.

'Godzilla featured a dinosaur as did King Kong,' Mrs Dawson continued.

'I've seen King Kong,' I said. 'The original version, that is.'

'Faye Wray was lovely, wasn't she, dear?' said Mrs Dawson. 'Although I did feel sorry for the monkey.'

Staring out of the window, I imagined King Kong running amok along Winslow Place before climbing to the top of the church tower holding Miss Taylor from the library, growling as several bi-planes fired machine-guns at him before he fell, with a crash, on Mr Bishop's recently over-polished Ford Anglia. Suddenly, I felt sorry for 'the monkey' too.

I picked up the tv guide. It wasn't a particularly interesting one but came free with the newspaper. It had everything I needed to know about future programmes as well as reviews of the latest books.

'Rear Window with James Stewart is on the tv this afternoon,' I said. 'Do you fancy watching it?'

'That would be lovely, dear,' replied Mrs Dawson, running her finger around the edge of the place mat.

We both looked across to Norman Drudge's window. He was sat, looking forward, drinking a cup of tea. He looked quite smart in his pale coloured Chinos and his open-necked short-sleeved shirt. He had a look of an office worker, even on his day off.

'Is that the one where James Stewart becomes obsessed with his neighbour?' Mrs Dawson asked.

'Yes,' I replied.

I'd seen the film at least twenty times, several times

173

with Mrs Dawson, and knew every scene and practically the whole script. Even so, I still enjoyed it.

'It's not very true to life, is it, dear?' said Mrs Dawson, as we watched Norman intently. He picked up his binoculars and gazed across the street.

'I love it,' I said. 'Apart from Some Like It Hot, I think that it's my favourite film of all time. Oh, and It's A Wonderful Life.'

'Perhaps, you should invite Paul over some time to watch an old movie,' suggested Mrs Dawson.

'I'm not sure it would be his thing,' I said. 'He probably likes more modern films. Special effects, monsters, aliens and the like.'

'You never know,' said Mrs Dawson. 'There's no better actor than James Stewart.'
She was right, of course. I could watch James Stewart movies all day.

'Alf used to do a blinding impression of him,' said Mrs Dawson, laughing. 'He could be very funny at times.'
I imagined the Alf I'd seen in an old photograph in a gilt frame on Mrs Dawson's mantlepiece doing an impression of the laconic actor. It was hard to picture. I poured the tea into our china cups and we stared out on to the street.

'It's very quiet today,' said Mrs Dawson. 'You would think that more people would be milling about on a Sunday. You never see kids out on the streets nowadays, do you?'

'Maybe there's a football match on the television or something,' I said.
I knew little about sport. It might not have even been the football season. Mrs Dawson looked at me intently for a few seconds.

'You look tired, dear,' said Mrs Dawson. 'Have you been sleeping alright? Your eyes look very black.' I hadn't noticed but decided to check myself out in the bathroom mirror once Mrs Dawson had left. Was it really that obvious that I hadn't been sleeping? Dr Wilson at the local surgery had once prescribed sleeping tablets but I hadn't taken them after Mrs Walters said that they'd left her acting like a zombie. The thought of Mrs Walters roaming the streets at night, attacking random pedestrians with an axe, shot through my head. Anyway, Dr Wilson was a bit of a quack and I wasn't about to take his advice. I much preferred Dr Arscott but so did everyone else and getting an appointment with him was practically impossible. His receptionist was particularly precious about him and insisted on the ins and outs of any illness before she'd give me an appointment. I wouldn't have minded so much but the whole surgery could hear everything she said as she talked particularly loud while at the same time being very condescending.

'It's the fireworks,' I said. 'Didn't you hear them?'

'No, dear,' said Mrs Dawson. 'I've been putting earplugs in. I've been sleeping like a log. What time were they?'

'About 4am,' I replied.

'Alf had tinnitus, drove him mad,' said Mrs Dawson. 'He'd wake up some nights swearing he could hear brass bands.'

'Oh,' I said.

'As well as road drills, sleigh bells,' continued Mrs Dawson, 'and African bongo drums.'

'That sounds awful,' I said.

'Can you say 'bongo drums' any more, dear?'

asked Mrs Dawson. 'I'm not sure if it's racist.'

'I don't know,' I said. 'Can a drum be racist?' Mrs Dawson thought about it for a second while staring into her cup. She reminded me of a gypsy desperately trying to read someone's fortune in their tea leaves.

'You've got to be so careful nowadays,' she said. 'Phrases that were once commonplace are now frowned upon.'

'I know,' I said, as I watched Mr Bishop carry a bucket of water towards his car. It was too full and the water splashed onto the road as he walked leaving a wet trail from his house to his car.

'Anyway,' I continued. 'I know who's setting off the fireworks. I saw him when I got up.' Mrs Dawson looked up from her teacup.

'It's not Norman, is it?' she asked. 'He looks so quiet and placid.'

'No, it's not Norman,' I answered. 'It's little Sanjay from the shop.'

'Oh dear,' said Mrs Dawson. 'He's a bit young to be out at that time of the morning, isn't he?' Mrs Dawson had also noticed Mr Bishop and his bucket and watched him intently. He had a large, orange sponge and was lovingly washing the side of his car.

'I know,' I said. 'But should I tell Paul? I wouldn't want to get him into trouble. Perhaps I'll just wait until he gets bored with it.'

'But what if he does himself an injury?' said Mrs Dawson. 'Blows his hand off or something?'

We sipped our tea. My eyes were drawn to the wallpaper above the fridge which was peeling off in one corner. It had been put up long before I'd moved in and was a strange pink colour with white speckles. I imagined it had probably been red at one time when it was first hung, perhaps, in the 1980s, but it had long since faded, being hit daily by the strong sunlight streaming in through the adjacent window. I thought about replacing it. A nice yellow might look okay, perhaps. Maybe the landlord would give me some money towards it although he was particularly mean and his usual reply was, 'it looks alright to me.' I'd never hung wallpaper before, perhaps Mrs Dawson would help me. Her house was wallpapered in every room but I suppose Alf may have done that. Her back room had wood chip which was painted an odd brown colour. The charity shop had some odd rolls, not enough to do a whole room but perhaps enough to paper above the fridge.

'I suppose I should say something to Paul,' I said. 'I wouldn't want Sanjay to hurt himself.'

'And the neighbourhood would get some peace,' Mrs Dawson said, smiling as she reached into her handbag and pulled out a small notepad and pen.

'I need to get some onions,' she said. 'If I don't write it down, it'll go completely out of my head.' After writing down 'onions' she replaced the pad and pen back in her bag and put it down on the floor beside her feet. Mrs Dawson had particularly neat writing unlike mine which was scrawly and rushed. I'd tried writing 'properly' but it always looked a confused mess. I couldn't read it myself sometimes.

It was good having company in the flat. There was something about my conversations and time spent with Mrs Dawson that made me feel relaxed and calmer than I would normally. I would be lost without my regular visits. There was something about her drop ins that made me feel very cosy. It was true that I'd be

177

lost without her.

After we drank our tea, Mrs Dawson popped home to get her 'tv glasses'.

'It's all just a blur to me, dear,' she said. Her eyes hadn't been the same since she'd been diagnosed with glaucoma at a recent eye check at SpecSavers. Her name was on an NHS waiting list for an operation which she was dreading, although many months had passed since she had first been told.

'I must phone them up,' she'd said often but never did.

Mrs Dawson had several pairs of glasses including a pair for the cinema and a pair for reading.

'It's such a fuss,' said Mrs Dawson. 'You're lucky to have normal eyesight. I do miss it. That's age, I suppose. Don't ever get old, dear.'

It seemed a funny thing to say. Of course, one day I'd be Mrs Dawson's age. Would I have anyone to visit me or would I be one of those people I often saw on my way to work staring out of their windows with only a budgie for company, perhaps? I imagined myself old and lonely with Tweety-Pie chirping in the background, busily pecking at its mirror. The thought was starting to depress me so I tried to think of happier things, Mrs Dawson and me feeding the ducks or me and Paul walking around the allotments and watching the sunset.

Mrs Dawson returned at 2pm, her tv glasses safely in her handbag. She'd also managed to do some shopping in the time she'd been away.

'I bought some Swiss Roll,' she said, 'to have with our tea.'

I hadn't had Swiss Roll since I'd been a little girl. It reminded me of being sat at home with my parents, of sunny summer days spent in the garden, Dad mowing the lawn, Mum baking a pie and me searching for butterflies. Perhaps I'd romanticised my past but childhood was like that, wasn't it?

Mrs Dawson and I took our places on the sofa and I turned on the television. It was one of those old fashioned ones with a wood surround and round knobs that had to be turned to tune in the station. I'd bought it from the charity shop for £5 and didn't like to get rid of it. It was very old, maybe from the 1970s. Mrs Dawson said that I should get a new one, flat screen and 33 inches, Curry's had a special deal on, apparently, but I felt at home with my old telly. And, anyway, it seemed more suited to watching old movies on.

'Your television is so small,' said Mrs Dawson. 'It's like a portable, it's just as well I fetched my glasses.'

'It's 20 inches,' I said. 'I don't think that I could watch it any bigger. It would give me a headache.' Mrs Dawson ran her hand along the top of the wooden surround. It was in need of a clean. Particles of dust caught in the rays of the sun coming through the kitchen window and were visible in the air until a cloud blocked out the light streaming in. I could see that when it reappeared, the sun was going to hit the tv screen so I pulled the curtains across slightly.

'Alf and me had one just like it,' said Mrs Dawson. 'I forget what happened to it. Perhaps it broke and we got a new one, I don't remember. I'm surprised yours has lasted so long.'

'I like my old telly,' I said, bending down to switch it on.

'Alice and her husband have an 80 inch one,' said Mrs Dawson, 'but then they would. It fills up the whole wall. I'm glad when they leave it off, it makes me feel dizzy. Oh, and the noise. I feel sorry for the neighbours.'

'Oh,' I said. 'I don't think I could watch that. I'll stick with my out-of-date 20 inch one.'
Even the thought of Alice's television made me feel slightly off balance.

Mrs Dawson arranged the cushions on the couch 'to give her back support' and we both got comfortable. She suffered with her back and had been to the surgery several times. Dr Wilson had prescribed anti depressants which she hadn't taken.

'The man's a buffoon,' she'd said at the time. Anyway, after a few weeks rest and taking it easy, her back got better all on its own although she had slight twinge now and then, especially if she got up funny or carried too much shopping.

'I saw Paul,' said Mrs Dawson. 'He sends his love.'

'His love?' I asked.

'Well, he said something like that,' she said. 'He said that he'll pop around later.'

'Not during the film, I hope,' I joked.

'No, this evening, sometime,' Mrs Dawson replied. 'I hope you don't mind but I told him about Sanjay and the fireworks.'
There was an advert on the television showing a Labrador puppy playing with a toilet roll. I wondered what it would be like having a dog for company, although I imagined that my landlord wouldn't be too happy about it and anyway, I'm sure that it would be lonely and bored while I was at work. Maybe I could get a cat like Mr Peter's Malcolm. They seemed quite happy to make their own entertainment.

'Oh,' I said. 'I hope he doesn't get into too much trouble.'

'Paul seems pretty easygoing,' said Mrs Dawson, 'but I don't know what Sanjay's mother will make of it all.'

The film started. The Paramount Pictures emblem showing a snow-capped mountain appeared. I loved the beginning announcing that the film was in 'glorious technicolor' before the stars' names appeared on the screen.

'It's just like being at the pictures,' said Mrs Dawson. 'I'd forgotten that Grace Kelly was in it.'

'We've seen it loads of times,' I said.

'She married that Prince, the one in Monaco, he was far too old for her,' said Mrs Dawson. 'And short, he was very short. He wasn't particularly handsome either.'

'This is so much more exciting than modern films,' Mrs Dawson continued. 'Oh, and Ironside is in it also.'

'Ironside?' I asked.

'Him in the wheelchair, the tv detective,' replied Mrs Dawson. 'Now, what's his name? Oh yes, Raymond Burr. Perry Mason. He was gay, you know. Well, that's what Mrs Gregson said in the hairdressers.'

Sometimes my conversations with Mrs Dawson made little sense. The actor in the film didn't appear to have a wheelchair although James Stewart did.

'Watch out for Alfred Hitchcock,' she said. 'He's in all his films, lurking in the background somewhere.'

I was just relaxing and getting into the movie when Mrs Dawson shouted,

'There he is. There he is.'

A short, rotund man with a face like an upset bulldog could be seen winding a clock in the background.

'Did you see him?' asked Mrs Dawson.

'Yes, I saw him,' I replied.

We went through the same procedure every time we watched an Alfred Hitchcock film.

'Is this the one where he's scared of heights?' asked Mrs Dawson.

'No, that's Vertigo,' I replied.

'Oh, I thought we were watching that one,' said Mrs Dawson. 'What's this one about?

'It's the one about a man who's confined to a wheelchair and spends the long hot summer watching his neighbours from his window,' I said.

'Oh, yes,' said Mrs Dawson. 'I remember now. Is this on ITV or the BBC?'

'ITV,' I said.

'Good,' she said. 'We can put the kettle on during the break and have a slice of that Swiss Roll.'

'Okay,' I said.

I loved our afternoons indoors watching old movies but there was always a constant chatter from Mrs Dawson. At least she'd given up bringing her knitting. The clitter-clatter of the needles made it very hard to concentrate although she did once knit me a nice auburn scarf.

'When was this made?' asked Mrs Dawson.

'I don't know,' I replied. 'The 1950s, I suppose.' I reached down and picked up the tv guide and scanned the listings.

'1954,' I said.

Mrs Dawson watched as James Stewart wheeled his wheelchair to his apartment window.

'Hasn't the world changed since 1954?' she

182

announced.

'Yes,' I replied trying to concentrate on the plot even though I knew it off by heart.

The first part ended and the adverts came on.

'Shall we have that cup of tea now, dear?' asked Mrs Dawson, looking at the tv guide. 'Is Ray Milland not in this?'

'I think you're thinking of Dial M for Murder,' I said.

'Oh, good,' said Mrs Dawson. 'I never did like him much. Alf said that he had a look of our butcher. I couldn't see it myself.'

I put the kettle on and made some tea which we drank while eating the Swiss Roll that Mrs Dawson brought. It was sweeter than I remembered from when I'd had it as a child.

'This is lovely,' I said. 'An old film, a good friend and a piece of cake. What more could you want?'

Mrs Dawson left at 4pm and Paul came around shortly after 5pm. He looked slightly dismayed.

'I'm sorry about the fireworks and Sanjay,' he said. 'He's a good boy most of the time.'

'It's no problem,' I said. 'I hope he's not in too much trouble.'

'Devyani wasn't very happy with him or me,' said Paul. 'They were old stock, kept out the back from last November. I'd been meaning to get rid of them. I don't like throwing anything away that could come in handy. You never know when someone might want some fireworks for a birthday or something.'

'They're very noisy,' I said.

'I know,' said Paul. 'Both Mr and Mrs Patel have been cursing the person setting them off for the last week or so.'

183

'Sanjay will be in the doghouse,' I said.

'Mr and Mrs Patel have got him doing extra chores in the shop,' said Paul. 'He's not very happy. He's in there now.'

I felt guilty. Maybe I shouldn't have mentioned the firework culprit to Mrs Dawson.

'Why don't we fetch him,' I said, 'and take him up to the allotments? Cheer him up a bit.'

'I don't know,' said Paul. 'What would Devyani say?'

'She'd want him to be happy, I suppose,' I said.

I fetched my coat.

'If we go now, we can have a nice walk and then watch the sunset,' I said.

We met up with Sanjay. He was dolefully stocking the shelves with baked beans as Mr Patel Senior watched on.

'What would Devyani say?' said Mr Patel Senior when we told him of our plans to take Sanjay to the allotments but he soon smiled and said, 'Go on, take the boy and see if you can cheer him up a bit.'

Sanjay smiled up at me. He looked as if he might have been crying. His eyes were very red. I ran my hand through his dark mop of hair and gave it a quick ruffle. He laughed.

Chapter Sixteen

I felt anxious on Monday morning as I sat at the kitchen table eating my cornflakes gazing blankly out of the window. Wisps of smoke travelled along the street from some distant bonfire. Today was the day that I'd decided to apologise to Miss Taylor. Maybe it was easier just to ignore her as Mrs Dawson had suggested but I felt I had to say sorry, I had made her cry after all and I wasn't proud of myself for that.

I left the flat just after 8am, a slight breeze blew rubbish along the damp pavement. It included several empty bags of crisps and the front page of yesterday's Chronicle which featured a photo of Councillor Evans, grinning inanely, cutting a ribbon in front of a group of newly-built homes. I'd seen Mr Granger cleaning his front windows with newspaper the day before so I assumed it was his.

'At one time, everyone used newspapers to clean their windows,' Mrs Dawson had told me. 'It gives them a nice shine.'

I hadn't tried it and, anyway, it was difficult enough cleaning my windows, two floors up, without fiddling on with old newspapers.

I popped into Patel's on the way to work to buy some cakes for the staff's tea break. The door creaked loudly on its hinges as I entered the shop. It might be easier to apologise to Miss Taylor if she had a cream doughnut rammed in her mouth, I concluded.

Paul was busily setting up a display of baked beans into a precarious pyramid shape. They weren't Heinz beans but were some cheaper brand popular with corner shops and customers on a tight budget. They looked like they could tumble at any moment. Paul saw me and smiled.

'Hello, Gemma,' he said. 'What do you think? Only 19p a tin.'

There was a slight rocking as I moved closer to have a look. I'd never seen a pyramid of baked beans before.

'It looks impressive,' I said, 'but what if someone takes one? Won't they all collapse?'

'Oh,' said Paul. 'I hadn't thought of that.'

'How long has it taken you to build it?' I asked.

'Just this morning and a bit of yesterday evening,' he replied. 'They were selling off cheap at the wholesalers.'

The breeze from the door made the display wobble a bit more but they managed to stay in place. There was a slight rattling sound as the tins shifted slightly.

'Today's the day,' I said. 'The day I've decided to apologise to Miss Taylor.'

'Show her that you're the better person,' said Paul. 'What's the worst that could happen?'

I looked over to the counter where the array of doughnuts and other treats were displayed underneath a large plastic cover. The cover kept off hungry wasps and small prying hands.

186

'I thought that a cream horn might help,' I said. 'And a variety of cakes for the other staff.'

'Miss Taylor looks more like an iced finger sort of person,' said Paul. 'We've got some nice pink ones.' He produced a pair of silver-coloured tongs and put a selection of different cakes in a white box. I took a ten pound note out of my purse. It was the red leather one that Mrs Dawson had given me for my birthday.

'They're on the house,' said Paul. 'I hope they will help.'

I smiled and whispered a quiet 'thank you' as I took the box, slightly nudging the array of disposable lighters that stood near by. My clumsiness was renowned in the library and I made sure that I stayed well away from Paul's display.

'Will I see you tonight?' asked Paul. 'It looks like it's going to be another sunny evening.'

'Of course,' I replied. 'I'd like that very much.' Paul moved the display of disposable lighters back to where they were originally, just beside the till.

'I thought that we could have a walk around the allotments again,' said Paul. 'And watch the sunset over the fields.'

It sounded perfect. The allotments had suddenly became my favourite place to visit, after the duckpond, that is.

'I'll see you after work,' I said, as I made my way towards the shop's door. 'Bye.'

Paul smiled and waved as I left, the bell ringing in the slight breeze.

'Good luck,' he shouted before turning to see how he could re-arrange his pyramid of baked beans. I thought that I heard a loud bang as I walked away as if something had collapsed suddenly but I decided not to return to the shop and investigate. If Paul's display had imploded, I figured, he wouldn't want me standing around with a face that said, 'I told you so.'

There was a chill in the air as I made my way to work. It wasn't quite summer but already yellowed leaves were falling from the trees and gathering on the pavement. I walked quicker than normal, eager to get my apology over and done with. Mr Graves said a quiet, almost abrupt, 'Good morning' as I passed but I didn't stop to chat. He had an odd pair of tartan trousers on, the sort that professional golfers wore on the television. They looked quite out of place but I imagined that he must be going to some sort of function, one where tartan trousers were a requirement. I'd realised years ago that Mr Graves wasn't a 'chatty' sort of person. Not that I wanted to chat today anyway. I had something very important to get off my chest.

I reached the library, it was looking decidedly tatty outside. The two concrete plant pots which had been cemented either side of the entrance contained no plants but were full of discarded cigarette butts even though there was a sign nearby clearly saying 'No Smoking'. A squashed Coke tin lay close by, flattened by a passing car. Someone had sprayed an 'anarchy' symbol on the wall of the front of the library and an abandoned aerosol tin lay nearby, rolling about on the pavement whenever the wind caught it. I picked the aerosol can and Coke tin up and put them in the nearby plastic bin which had been supplied by the council but had a hole in the side, the shape of a size ten boot. The wooden bench beside it had seem better days with many of its struts rotten and looking like they could collapse at any moment. At one end, someone had used a disposable barbecue which left a black sooty square

188

mark. Rubbish from the outdoor meal lay underneath the seat, spilling across the pavement. The seat really needed replacing but the council were strapped for cash and reluctant to put money into anything connected with the soon-to-be closed nearby amenity.

I walked through the automatic doors of the library feeling quite uncomfortable. They had been recently oiled but let out a loud squeaking noise every time they opened or closed, announcing my presence as soon as I arrived. It was very quiet inside. I could see Callum busily putting returned books back on the shelves. He had a new t-shirt, a bright yellow colour, with a slogan which read, 'No Nukes is Good Nukes.' Brian had a clipboard and pen and seemed to be carrying out some sort of inventory. An overweight man was busily eyeing up the new food and drink automated machine by the doorway which had recently been delivered. It sold lots of chocolate treats as well as a range of sandwiches, all carefully wrapped in secure cardboard and cellophane wrappers. Callum had become a regular visitor, pumping endless coins into the machine to get various pre-packaged treats.

Mr Peters was at the front desk checking through listings on the computer. He looked up and smiled.

'Hello, Gemma,' he said. 'Feeling better?'
I looked quickly towards the Men's Health section and then back towards Mr Peters. His ornate moustache looked particularly spruce today.

'Much better,' I said. 'Is Miss Taylor about?'
Mr Peters looked quickly around the library, seeing if he could see her hiding away anywhere.

'She was here a second ago,' he said. 'I think that she's probably somewhere in the music section.'
I decided it was now or never so I headed towards the

music section to offer Miss Taylor my apology. I had to get it off my chest and then everything could get back to normal. I could be my usual, polite, calm self and Miss Taylor could be condescending and aloof. Normal service would be resumed.

Only it wasn't that easy. Miss Taylor wasn't in the music section. I assumed if she wasn't there, she would be with the other 'witch', Cecilia Moorhouse. They were probably plotting, scheming on ways to get their own back or working out ways to get me dismissed.

I walked up the polished wooden steps leading up to the reference library and peered in through the window. Miss Moorhouse was sat there, busily scribbling down notes from the library's microfiche machine. Anything could go on in the world around her when she was glued to that machine and she wouldn't notice. I'd tried talking to her in the past when she was writing down notes but my comments just went unanswered. I was way down Cecilia's list of importance.

There was no sign of Miss Taylor. I carried on along the landing and into the staffroom and there she was, sat on a chair, one of those bright orange ones, leaning forwards with her head in her hands. My heart rate quickened and my hands felt clammy. She looked up. She had a strained look, a look as if she hadn't been able to sleep for days. Her eyes looked black and hollow.

'Gemma,' she said. She'd never called me Gemma ever in all the time I'd worked there. I felt slightly unnerved.

'Gemma, I'm so sorry,' she continued. 'I've been a complete and utter cow.'

There was no arguing with her statement but I felt I had to apologise too, if only to clear the air. It wouldn't be an admission that I actually liked her.

'I'm sorry too,' I said.

'You've got nothing to be sorry for,' she said. 'I realise what I'm like.'

'But I am sorry,' I said.

She smiled. She seemed to have more teeth than a normal person but perhaps that was just my imagination. I don't think I'd ever seen her smile before. It was almost unsettling and, for a split second, she reminded me of the shark in the movie, Jaws. I could hear the soundtrack in my head with its approaching sense of doom. Dun-dun, dun-dun, dun-dun, dun-dun...

'I bought you these,' she said, producing a large bunch of flowers from underneath the chair.

They were beautiful and looked expensive. They certainly weren't a £2.99 bunch from Patel's and looked like they come from a 'posh' flower shop in the town somewhere.

The image in my head that I was about to be devoured by a man-eating shark quickly disappeared.

'That's very kind of you,' I said as I took the flowers and gently sniffed them. For a second, I had visions of being pricked by a thorn and sleeping for 100 years but Miss Taylor wasn't really a witch. Was she?

'I hope we can get on,' she said. 'We've only probably got a couple more weeks working together. And then, after that, who knows?'

She got up to leave. She stood up straight as if a great burden had been lifted off her shoulders. Her black eye mascara was slightly smudged but I didn't think that it would be polite to tell her. I suddenly saw her in a new light. I didn't particularly like her and I'm sure that we would never be friends but at least she'd tried.

'I bought some cakes. For our break,' I said. 'I got you a cream horn.'

Miss Taylor smiled, as if in appreciation and left the room. I placed the flowers in the sink and looked around for something to place them in to give them a drink and to show them off. I didn't want them to die before I got them home. An old coffee jar made an ideal, if somewhat small, makeshift vase. I placed the flowers in the window so that everyone could see them. The sunlight shone through the yellow petals casting a shadow on the opposite wall. The reflected shadow on the far wall danced with the breeze coming in through the slightly opened window.

Mr Peters was still at the front desk when I returned downstairs. Someone had left a large splodge of chewing gum stuck on the corner of the counter. I picked at it with my finger nails, nervously, trying to remove it.

'Is everything alright?' Mr Peters asked, 'With Miss Taylor, that is.'

'She gave me a lovely bunch of flowers,' I said, 'and I bought her a cream horn.'

He looked up and watched Miss Taylor walking back towards the music section. She looked happier than he'd seen her in a long time.

'Oh,' he replied. 'Well I'm glad we're all on good terms again. I know that she can be hard work at times.'

'Yes,' I answered but said no more. I wanted to forget the whole argument.

It was quiet all morning. I was hoping that a

few more people would come through the doors, if only to show that the library was popular. Nigel Wain came in at about 10am to peruse the library's copy of The Guardian and I watched as he read it in a quiet corner of the History section, his nose pressed right up against the page. I wondered what was wrong with his eyesight but I didn't like to ask. And, anyway, it was none of my business. I made him a cup of coffee at about 10.20am in his little china cup. He was grateful, as always, but said little. No-one objected to me making him coffee today especially not Miss Taylor who appeared jollier than I'd seen her in a long time. Nigel also got a ginger nut which he seemed very grateful for.

At 11pm, we all sat down and had a cup of tea and ate the cakes that I'd got earlier at Patel's. Miss Moorhouse had a pink iced finger, Callum had a jam doughnut, Brian had a chocolate doughnut, Mr Peters had a cream doughnut and, of course, Miss Taylor had her cream horn. She did her best to look as if she was enjoying it but seemed slightly embarrassed by the mess she was making. I imagined her eating one at home with a silver teaspoon. I thought that some of the cream doughnut that Mr Peters had, might have got lodged in his moustache but he'd had his hairy attachment so long that he was used to eating all manner of foods without causing a mess.

'Does anyone know what they might do when the library closes?' he asked.
There were a few seconds silence which wasn't a bad thing for a library, I suppose.

'I might see if I can get a job with the council,' said Brian. 'Filing and such like. I don't suppose that it would be much different from working in the library.' He seemed well suited to it. He had a fussy, office

193

worker sort of way about him. Not in an annoying way, he was just very tidy and methodical about anything he did.

'A place for everything,' he'd say often, 'and everything in its place.'

'I've filled in a form for a job working at The Final Frontier,' said Callum.

He'd obviously dismissed his former idea of becoming a butcher's apprentice. I was pleased. He was more suited to being around nerdy Dr Who and Star Trek fans than he was being around dead animals.

'Miss Moorhouse?' asked Mr Peters.

'Oh, I don't know,' she replied. 'Perhaps I'll continue to research family trees, from home, that is. There's a lot of call for it. A laptop and a subscription to Ancestry.com is all that's needed.'

'I hope to get a job at the Central Library,' said Miss Taylor. 'If they'll have me, that is.'

Mr Peters smiled and looked over to me.

'And what about you, Gemma,' he asked.

'Oh, that's easy,' I replied. 'I'm going to marry Mr Patel and work in the corner shop.'

I don't know what made me blurt it out. I suddenly felt very confident about things after resolving my problems with Miss Taylor. There was a look of surprise on everyone's face especially on that of Cecilia Moorhouse.

'Good for you,' said Miss Taylor.

She was slowly growing on me.

Nobody said much more after that. It was almost as if me mentioning my future plans had somehow completely killed the conversation. We drank our tea, ate our cakes and slowly drifted off back to work.

Mrs Dawson came into the library at 12.30pm.

She had with her her tartan shopping trolley on wheels. It had seen better days, it was at least thirty years old and had a small hole in the bottom that Mrs Dawson has expertly darned.

'I might do some shopping later,' she said. 'Just bits.'
She said that she was looking for a copy of Jamaica Inn but we both knew that she was there to see if I was alright.

'How are things with Miss Taylor?' she asked.

'She bought me a lovely bunch of flowers,' I replied, edging a ruler against the piece of chewing gum which had now hardened. 'They're in the staffroom. They look very expensive.'

'Oh,' said Mrs Dawson, looking surprised. 'You know when someone's feeling guilty when they buy you flowers. Alf never bought me flowers.'
I wasn't sure if that was a good or bad thing.

'He never bought you flowers?' I asked.

'Well, only once,' she replied. 'When he knocked over and smashed my Siamese cat and mouse ornament. He felt very guilty, he even tried gluing it back together. Most of the glue ended up on his hands. He made a right mess. Two of his fingers got stuck together, we nearly had to go to the A&E department of the hospital.'

'Oh,' I said. 'And now you have a replacement.'

'Yes and it reminds me so much of Alf,' she said smiling. 'Thank you, dear.'
I was pleased that I'd made her happy.

'Have you seen Paul today?' Mrs Dawson asked.

'Yes,' I replied. 'I saw him this morning. He gave me some lovely cakes for the staff. Miss Taylor had a cream horn.'

Mrs Dawson looked over disapprovingly towards Miss Taylor.

'I bet she did,' she said.

Miss Taylor saw Mrs Dawson looking at her and smiled and gave her a small wave. Mrs Dawson waved back, uncomfortably, and returned the smile before turning back to me.

'What's wrong with her?' she asked.

'I think that she's trying to turn over a new leaf,' I said.

'Hmm,' replied Mrs Dawson. 'We'll see. A leopard never changes its spots.'

I shifted a large pile of books, erratically stacked on top of each other, to one side so that I could see Mrs Dawson more easily.

'We're going for a walk around the allotments this evening,' I said. 'Perhaps you and Mr Raman would like to come?'

Mrs Dawson looked uncomfortable.

'I've not seen Mr Raman since our restaurant date,' she said. 'Maybe it's not a good idea to get too close.'

Mrs Dawson's eyes were drawn to me continually pushing Mr Peter's metal ruler against the chewing gum. It was no good, it wouldn't move.

'You want a razor blade for that,' she said. 'It's a filthy habit, chewing gum, isn't it dear? And it makes such a mess of things. You can barely see the pavement at the precinct for it.'

I gave up and placed Mr Peter's ruler back in the tall pot he used to store his pens, pencils and scissors in.

'Have you phoned him?' I asked. 'Mr Raman, that is.'

196

'No,' replied Mrs Dawson. 'Although the phone has rung once or twice but I haven't answered it. You know what I'm like with telephones.'

Mrs Dawson had one of those old-fashioned home phones that had a dial on it. It had originally been new in 1972 and was an odd yellow sort of colour. A colour that reminded me of Coleman's mustard.The receiver was very heavy and dialling was a long and laborious job.

'Why don't you get a more modern one?' I'd asked her one time.

'You know me,' she'd said. 'I never use it anyway. What's the point of getting a new one and, anyway, it's like part of the furniture. It's always been there and probably always will be. That is, of course, until I die, I suppose. Then you can have it. It will be collectable by then.'

Mrs Dawson hated speaking on the phone and barely ever picked it up. I wondered why she even had one.

'Whoever's that?' she'd say whenever I was at her house and the phone rang. She'd never answer it.

'I don't want to get stuck talking to some salesman all day,' she'd say. 'Asking me about PPI and suchlike. I don't even know what PPI is.'

She always phoned 1471 straight after a call and if it was a number she recognised, like mine, she'd phone back.

'But you like him, don't you?' I said. 'Mr Raman, that is?'

'Yes,' replied Mrs Dawson. 'But I'm married to Alf.'

'But Alf's dead,' I said.

As soon as the words left my lips, I wished that I hadn't said them. The last thing I wanted to do was upset Mrs

Dawson.

'I know, dear,' she said. 'But it somehow doesn't seem right. It's almost as if I'm brushing Alf to one side as if I never knew him and that upsets me greatly.'

'But you like Mr Raman,' I said. 'Don't let it pass you by. I'm sure that Alf would have wanted you to be happy.'

'I know, I know,' said Mrs Dawson. 'I'll have to give the matter more thought.'

A man dropped a book in the Oversized Books section and it hit the floor with a loud thud that seemed to echo throughout the building. He quickly picked it up and waved across shouting, 'Sorry.'

I gave a quiet, nervous wave back and mouthed, 'It's okay.'

I changed the subject. I could see that Mrs Dawson was uneasy talking about Mr Raman.

'I thought that Mr Peters would get his moustache lost in his cream doughnut,' I said.

'If I was married to him,' said Mrs Dawson. 'I'd make him cut it off.'

She reached for the scissors and snipped through thin air as she pretended to cut off the ends of Mr Peter's Dahliesque attachment.

She looked over to Miss Taylor who was busily searching the shelves in the history section looking for a book for a customer.

'Have you heard any more about the closure of the library?' asked Mrs Dawson.

'It's all gone quiet,' I said. 'I suppose we'll be amalgamated with the Central Library and that will be it.'

Mrs Dawson sighed.

'Mr Peters asked everyone what they intended

to do when the library closes and I said that I plan to marry Paul and work in the shop,' I said. 'It just came out. I don't know what made me say it.'

'Oh,' said Mrs Dawson. 'I wouldn't worry about it. I'm sure they probably weren't listening. Anyway, that would be lovely.'

'What would?' I asked.

'You marrying Paul,' said Mrs Dawson.

'But we hardly know each other,' I replied. Mrs Dawson shifted around some left notices and papers that were on the counter and put them into a tidy pile.

'I see that Lidls are selling inflatable kayaks,' she said, reading a leaflet that had been left on the counter. 'That's not much use to you or me, is it?'

'No,' I replied, wondering why she'd mentioned it.

'Avocados are only 69p,' she said. 'I'm not sure I've ever had an avocado.'

She read the leaflet from top to bottom, turned it over and then placed it back on the counter.

'Oh, well, I suppose I should search for Jamaica Inn,' she said.

'I could find it for you,' I replied.

'It's okay, dear,' said Mrs Dawson. 'I like a good look around. You never know what you might find.'

As Mrs Dawson headed for the fiction section, Norman Drudge entered the library. He saw me at the front desk and came over.

'Hello again,' he said.

'Hello,' I said. 'How are the dormice?'

'Fine,' he said, 'although someone keeps letting off fireworks. It plays havoc with the wildlife.'

'Oh,' I said. 'That's odd.'

I didn't want to say any more as I didn't want to get Sanjay into more trouble than he was in already.

'Is Mr Peters around?' asked Norman.

I looked around and saw Mr Peters in the geography section. He seemed deeply engrossed in an oversized book about the tribes of West Africa. A man with an ornate headdress and a spear adorned the cover.

'Mr Peters,' I shouted. 'Mr Williams is here to see you.'

Someone in the background shouted 'Shhh!', something I hadn't heard in the library for many years. Mr Peters looked over and instead of shouting, I mimed with my hands, as best as I could, that Norman wanted to see him.

Mr Peters left what he was doing and quickly came to the front desk.

'Ah, Mr Williams,' said Mr Peters. 'How can I help you?'

Mr Peters smiled as if he was happy to see Norman. They shook hands. It was a very quick handshake, not one of those long clammy handshakes, the type that Councillor Evans gave to everyone he met.

'Is there somewhere where we could talk in private?' asked Norman.

It all sounded very ominous.

'We could talk in the staffroom,' said Mr Peters, edging Norman in the general direction with his left hand.

I watched them climb the polished wooden stairs, go into the staffroom and close the door behind themselves. I wondered what they would make of the bunch of flowers that Miss Taylor had given me, displayed beautifully on the window ledge. I wondered

200

if perhaps they'd have a cup of tea and whose mug they would drink from. Mr Peters had his own mug but whose would he give to Norman? Not Miss Moorhouse's stained one, I hoped. I suppose Mr Peters would give Norman his cup of tea in my special china cup and saucer, the one reserved for special guests.

Mrs Dawson returned with a dog-eared version of Jamaica Inn.

'It's been well-read,' she said. 'But I suppose it's very popular.'

'Mr Peters was going to order some more,' I replied, 'but with the forthcoming closure, he hasn't been able to.'

Mrs Dawson looked quickly around the library.

'Was that Norman I saw at the desk a couple of minutes ago?' she asked. 'He looked a bit flustered, didn't he?'

I picked up the copy of Jamaica Inn and scanned it. It took several goes but the machine finally let out a loud beep.

'He wanted a private word with Mr Peters,' I said. 'They're in the staffroom right now.'

We both turned and stared in the general direction. The door was tightly shut and there was no sign of movement. Miss Moorhouse walked quickly by the staffroom on her way to the reference library but didn't stop to investigate. She wasn't a nosy sort of person, too aloof to let anyone know that she might be interested in their lives.

'I wonder what he wants?' asked Mrs Dawson.

I picked up a pen and slowly chewed on the end. It was a disgusting habit, I know, but better than biting my finger nails, I assumed.

'Probably finalising a date for the closure,' I

said as I moved the pen around my mouth like a cowboy chewing a matchstick. I realised that it wasn't a good look and took it out of my mouth and placed it in amongst Mr Peter's other writing implements.

'And then I'll be unemployed,' I continued. Mrs Dawson's looked towards the half-chewed pen before looking back at me.

'You'd better marry Mr Patel quickly,' she joked.

As we were talking and I was flicking through the pages of Mrs Dawson's book, I saw Norman and Mr Peters coming out of the staffroom and heading down the stairs. Norman left quickly by the front door as if he had an urgent meeting to attend. Mr Peters approached the desk.

'There's a meeting at the Guildhall tomorrow at 11am to discuss and maybe prevent the closure of the library,' said Mr Peters.

Before I could respond, Mrs Dawson spoke up.

'Tomorrow at 11am?' she said. 'Are the general public invited?'

Mr Peters placed a cardboard folder, which he had been carrying under his arm, on to the counter. He hadn't had it when he went into the staffroom and I wondered what it contained.

'Everyone is invited, especially you, Mrs Dawson,' he replied.

Mrs Dawson let out a short sigh. It was the sort of a sigh a child might make if you gave him cabbage for his tea.

'But how will anyone know about it?' asked Mrs Dawson.

Mr Peters raised his eyebrows. The action made the ends of his well-waxed moustache move up and down slightly. I became fascinated by it but didn't want him to catch me looking.

'Maybe that's the council's plan,' said Mr Peters. 'To brush the matter under the carpet as quickly as possible.'

'And Norman? I mean Mr Williams?' Mrs Dawson inquired.

'He's doing his best to help us,' replied Mr Peters. 'By keeping us informed.'

'Well, he's a bit late, isn't he, dear?' replied Mrs Dawson.

Mr Peters looked around the library to see where the other members of staff were. They had all scuttled off to various parts of the library and were nowhere to be seen.

'I'm going to get Miss Moorhouse and Miss Taylor to print up some leaflets,' said Mr Peters, 'and then perhaps the staff could distribute them through nearby doors, to passersby and anyone in general.'

'I'm happy to help,' I said although it sounded like an impossible task. 'Maybe we could have some pinned up in shops?'

Mrs Dawson picked up her book and placed it carefully in her trolley. She looked slightly disgruntled.

'It's a bit late in the day,' she said. 'It will take several hours just organising it all.'

Mr Peters twiddled the right end side of his moustache between his finger and thumb. It somehow made him look more intelligent but I wasn't altogether sure why this was.

'Well, it's all we can do for now,' he said, as he left to tell the other members of the staff of his plan.

'I still have the leaflet from the last meeting,' said Mrs Dawson. 'A few alterations and I could take it to the printer's and get several hundred flyers made up quickly.'

I looked up at the clock. It was almost 1.30pm. It was worth a go.

With a bottle of Tippex and a marker pen, we changed the leaflet so it read:

'Stop the Library Closure. Meeting at The Guildhall on Tuesday at 11am. All welcome. Tell your friends.'

'Should it be a small 't' or a capital one before 'Guildhall', I asked.

'I don't suppose it matters, dear,' replied Mrs Dawson. 'No-one's going to be checking us for our punctuation.'

It wasn't much of a leaflet but said all it had to. I added the number of the library and also the number of the council offices before placing the leaflet on the photocopier to see what it would turn out like. It looked okay so I printed out five copies.

'I'll get my coat and come with you,' I said.

'What about the library?' asked Mrs Dawson.

'It's closing anyway,' I said. 'And I'm sure they can cope.'

We left the library. The automatic doors groaned as if they were going to stop working very shortly. As we walked across Portland Road, we saw two familiar faces coming towards us. It was Mr Patel Senior and Mr Raman.

Mr Raman smiled at Mrs Dawson. He was obviously pleased to see her.

'I hope I haven't upset you in some way,' he said. 'I haven't heard from you at all.'

Mrs Dawson looked embarrassed as if she was uneasy that other people could hear their conversation.

'You haven't upset me,' she said. 'It's just, I'm not used to being escorted by another man who isn't my husband. There was Mr Johnson, of course, but that was different.'

'I understand,' said Mr Raman. 'But we're still friends?'

'Of course,' said Mrs Dawson, not wanting to say more with Mr Patel Senior and myself standing close by.

I could see that Mrs Dawson was feeling uncomfortable so I changed the subject.

'We're on our way to the printer's,' I said. 'There's a meeting at the Guildhall tomorrow at 11am and we need to get some leaflets printed and distributed.'

Mr Patel Senior took a leaflet and stared intensely at it.

'We could help,' he said. 'The family could deliver and hand them out.'

'The more the merrier,' said Mrs Dawson. 'But we'll have to be quick. Can we all meet back here at 3pm?'

'Of course,' replied Mr Patel Senior.

Mr Raman gave Mrs Dawson a friendly smile and she looked down like a shy sixteen year old before looking up and returning the smile.

We headed off to the printer's walking briskly all the way. Mrs Dawson pulled along her trolley steadily which hit every bump and pothole in the pavement. It had seen better days.

'I don't think my heart's up to this,' Mrs Dawson joked.

Quickie Print was a good half a mile away but we made it by 1.50pm and were promised one thousand leaflets by 2.30pm.

We sat in the park as we waited. The ducks bothered us for some scraps but as we had none, they soon disappeared. The randy duck, I think it was the same one, pecked me hard in the leg before leaving. It was as if he was saying, 'Next time, make sure you come with some bread.'

'He is handsome,' said Mrs Dawson. 'And he's charming also. He's the perfect gentleman. Like an Indian James Mason or Cary Grant, perhaps.'
She was still thinking about Mr Raman and felt that she had, in some way, let him down.

'So what's the problem?' I said. 'You've always told me to grasp every opportunity. You wouldn't want me to ignore Paul, would you?'

'Of course not, dear,' she replied. 'But it's different. I'm an old woman, a silly old woman some would say, and perhaps too long in the tooth to be involved in a new romance.'

'Of course you're not too old,' I said.

'But it's different for you,' continued Mrs Dawson. 'You're a young girl. You've never lost someone you've been close to.'
I'd lost both my grandparents and had been close to them but I knew what Mrs Dawson meant. I'd never lost a long term partner. Mrs Dawson didn't want people to think that Mr Raman was somehow a replacement for Alf.
We gazed out across the pond. A lone jogger in tight red Lycra was running nearby.

'What does he think he looks like,' said Mrs Dawson. 'You can see all his bits and everything.'
I didn't know what to say as Mrs Dawson watched him run by. He noticed us and shouted a friendly 'Good afternoon.' Mrs Dawson looked back at him as if he'd

just arrived from Mars.

'The world's changed,' said Mrs Dawson. 'I couldn't imagine a time when Alf would have run around the park in a tight red costume showing off his all to all and sundry.'

I looked down. Remnants of bread lay at my feet.

'It's not right,' she said. 'Imagine if I ran around in tight red Lycra.'

The image in my head brought a slight smile to my face which I tried to hide because it seemed that Mrs Dawson was upset. I didn't want her to think that I was laughing at her.

I knew why she was getting annoyed. She was angry at herself for ignoring Mr Raman.

'We should get going,' I said. 'We'll pick up the leaflets and head back.'

We arrived at the library just after 3pm. Mrs Dawson had put the leaflets in her tartan trolley on wheels and we took it in turns pulling it back. One thousand leaflets were heavier than we thought they would be. I felt very old and a bit of an oddball as I pulled the trolley along. I had never realised the strange looks people with wheel trolleys got, almost as if there was something weird about the person pulling it.

Mr Patel Senior was waiting at the library with ten young boys, one of whom was Sanjay.

'Who are all these?' asked Mrs Dawson, smiling at Sanjay.

'Relatives,' replied Mr Patel Senior. 'Cousin's children, sons, nephews, grandchildren. They're all here to help.'

Sanjay smiled up at me. He always had a wide grin and sparkling eyes. I think he liked me and I'd forgiven him for the firework incident.

'I've drawn up a map,' said Mr Raman, 'so we make sure that we deliver to different areas.'

Mr Raman had worked in a drawing office for a firm of architects so I suppose drawing maps came naturally to him. He'd marked the name of each young boy on the map, colour coding the area that they had to cover. It was all very efficient.

'And I've emailed notices to all the shops in the area,' said Mr Patel Senior, 'asking them to print out the notice and place it in their windows.'

I hadn't imagined Mr Patel Senior sending emails or even using a computer.

'Paul would have liked to have been here,' continued Mr Patel Senior, 'but he's got to run the shop. He said that he'll see you this evening though.'

I was sort of pleased that Paul hadn't come. We might have spent too much time talking rather than hand mailing flyers.

'Are we delivering our leaflets together, dear?' Mrs Dawson asked.

I wanted her company but thought that she might want to rekindle her relationship with Mr Raman. She knew what I was about to say but before I could get the words out she spoke.

'It will be nice us delivering the leaflets together,' she said. 'We can chat about things, it will make it all a lot easier.'

Mr Raman and Mr Patel Senior distributed the leaflets amongst the boys which meant we had about seventy each.

'Perhaps we should have got more,' said Mrs Dawson but it was too late to do anything about it.

'It will have a knock-on effect,' said Mr Raman. 'A person receiving a leaflet might tell five friends and they might tell five more friends and so on.'

'I hope so,' replied Mrs Dawson. 'All we can do is try.'

She was right. What did we have to lose? We split up. Our round was easy enough. It covered Winslow Place, both sides, which meant afterwards we could return to my flat for a well-earned cup of tea.

We posted most of the leaflets through people's front doors. From the racket behind some of them, I was sure that several were eaten by angry dogs, annoyed that their owners had gone to work leaving them at home. I handed a leaflet to Mr Graves, the ex-policeman, who was out on the pavement presumably looking for our unpleasant postman.

'He gets later every day,' he grumbled. I handed him one of the leaflets.

'What's this,' he asked, looking at the flyer as if he'd never quite seen anything so disgusting.

'We're trying to save the library,' I said. 'There's a meeting at the Guildhall tomorrow morning.'

'Oh,' said Mr Graves, as he read it more slowly.

'Will you be able to attend?' I asked.

'I'll have to see what Mrs Graves has to say,' he replied. 'I'll try.'

As we walked away, Mrs Dawson sighed.

'She'll probably just throw that in the bin,' she said. 'She's the sort.'

Mrs Dawson's tartan trolley was giving up the will to live. One of its wheels had become slightly buckled which made steering difficult.

Mr Bishop polished his car in the distance.

'Hello, ladies,' he said. 'What's this?'

He dropped the cloth he was using into a grey plastic bucket which also contained a sponge and a tin of

209

Turtlewax.

'We're trying to save the library,' said Mrs Dawson, handing him the leaflet. 'It would be lovely if you could attend.'

'Tomorrow? I'll do my best,' replied Mr Bishop, 'but I've so much to do.'

He wiped his finger along a line of wax on his car that he hadn't rubbed in.

As we walked back to my flat, Mrs Dawson muttered.

'The man's an idiot,' she said. 'All he does is clean that car.'

With all the leaflets delivered, we got back to the flat at 4.30pm. Mrs Dawson rested her trolley up against the pedal bin in the kitchen. The bin opened as the trolley touched the pedal revealing all my discarded rubbish.

'I think I'll have to get another,' she said. 'Are there any in the charity shop?'

'I'll keep a look-out,' I said. 'Cup of tea?'

'That would be lovely, dear,' she said, as she leaned back on the couch. There were indentations in each end of the couch where we regularly sat. I really needed to get a new one but it was, however, comfortable.

I plugged in the kettle and got our two favourite china cups and saucers out of the cupboard.

'I do hope that I haven't upset Mr Raman,' said Mrs Dawson. 'I'll give him a ring later.'

'He'll be glad to hear from you,' I said.

'I suppose it's like that film,' said Mrs Dawson. 'The one with Peter Sellers and Sophie Loren. You know.'

'I don't think I've seen it,' I said.

Mrs Dawson started to sing.

'Doctor, I'm in trouble. Well, goodness

210

gracious me,' she sang in an odd Indian accent.

'Oh, no,' she said. 'I suppose that would be considered racist nowadays.'

'I suppose it would,' I replied.

'Peter Sellers plays an Indian gentleman,' said Mrs Dawson. 'Rather an odd choice, don't you think?'

'Yes,' I replied but I could only think of Peter Sellers as Inspector Clouseau in The Pink Panther.

'I saw the film at The Odeon in 1960 with Alf,' Mrs Dawson continued. 'What was it called now? I'm sure it started with 'M'.'

'Mousetrap?' I suggested.

'No, it wasn't that, dear,' replied Mrs Dawson. 'Ah, yes, of course, it was called The Millionairess.'

'I'll have to watch out for it,' I said, although it sounded like the sort of film that they wouldn't show nowadays.

'Of course, Mr Raman is nothing like Peter Sellers,' Mrs Dawson continued, 'and I'm certainly no Sophia Loren. Is she still alive, do you know?'

'I think so,' I replied.
I poured our tea out and we sat together on the couch staring towards the painting of Kynance Cove in Cornwall that I'd bought in the charity shop for 30p.

'There's another James Stewart film on on Sunday afternoon,' said Mrs Dawson. 'Shall I come around and we could watch it together?'

'That would be lovely,' I said. 'Which one is it?'

'It's a Wonderful Life,' said Mrs Dawson. 'The one with the angel, Gabriel. It always makes me cry.'

'It's a date,' I joked.

Chapter Seventeen

Mr Peters had phoned all the staff the previous evening saying that the library was to be shut all Tuesday so that we could attend the meeting at the Guildhall.

I wondered if all the leaflets had been successfully delivered and how many people would turn up. I wasn't hopeful.

I got up at 8am and had my cornflakes as usual, at the kitchen table. My friendly blackbird was nowhere to be seen. Perhaps he'd found another lonely soul who was more in need of his company than I was. Norman wasn't in his window either. Probably preparing for the meeting, I assumed.

It seemed odd being at home on a Tuesday morning. I could have read or watched something on the television but couldn't settle to do either. Was this what it was going to be like when I finally lost my job? How was I going to pay the rent? The job at Patels and my imagined marriage to Paul were all just a pipe dream.

I craned my neck to see Mr Bishop cleaning his car but

he wasn't there. I needed some reassurance, reassurance that this day was just like any other but, somehow, it wasn't.

Both Mrs Dawson and Paul called for me at 10am. It seemed odd having two visitors at once.

'Look who I bumped into,' said Mrs Dawson, smiling. She gazed over to the sink to see if it was full of unwashed dishes from the night before. It wasn't. I know that Mrs Dawson was concerned that I was looking after myself properly. I'd sometimes catch her out of the corner of my eye tidying up around behind me, putting away books and magazines and putting dirty clothes in the washing machine. I tried to only put the washing machine on once a week as it shook violently as it worked and had a tendency to walk around the kitchen. The people downstairs, the Bryants', got particularly annoyed with this and had banged on the ceiling in the past with the handle of a broom. I tried to do all my washing on a Thursday afternoon as the Bryants' seemed to go out then. They were a retired couple, maybe in their seventies, and didn't have time for many people especially me. Mrs Dawson had tried saying 'good morning' to them but their only conversation with her was moaning about my washing machine. I suppose I really should have got a new one. This one was at least twenty five years old and came with the flat.

I hadn't expected Paul to turn up with Mrs Dawson and I suddenly felt very untidy.

'I must look a mess,' I said. 'I just pulled on my old clothes.'

'You look beautiful,' said Paul. 'As always.'
I felt that he must be lying, but him just saying it made me suddenly feel a lot more positive.

Mrs Dawson looked down at her watch. It was a small watch with an expandable gold bracelet. The sort that left an indentation on your arm when you took it off. Alf had bought it for her on their twenty fifth wedding anniversary.

'I could never part with it,' she told me often. I had no watch. I felt that I didn't need one, always somehow knowing the exact time with uncanny accuracy.

'We really should be getting a move on,' said Mrs Dawson. 'We don't want to miss the beginning.' I grabbed my backpack. It was only a small one but was big enough to hold everything I needed; my keys, my money, a drink, some chocolate and room for the odd book or two. The front zipped-up pocket contained a mobile phone which I'd bought for £10 from Tesco. I wasn't really a mobile phone type of person and just carried it for emergencies. I'd see people on the street on the tube glued to their phones, oblivious to their surroundings, on a daily basis, narrowly missing being ran over by passing traffic or avoiding near disasters by a hair's breadth. Mrs Dawson felt the same as me about mobile phones.

'People miss out on so much,' she'd said. 'Always looking down, not seeing the beauty around them. If I had one, I'd jump on it.' She was right, of course.

I gazed over to the clock on the cooker. It had a digital red display which flashed on and off when you were least expecting it to and sometimes made a ringing noise. It was possible to exactly programme in the time it took to cook a meal, according to the handbook which came with it, but I'd never worked out how this was possible. Certainly, it could be very annoying at times, however, it kept good time, unlike the other appliances around the flat. They all told different times. I always relied on the cooker clock if I had an appointment or there was something on the television that I wanted to watch.

'I hope that I don't have to talk,' I said. 'They might want to know what the staff have to say about the closure.'

'I wouldn't worry about that,' said Mrs Dawson. 'I'm sure if anything needs saying on behalf of the staff, Mr Peters will say it. He somehow commands attention, with that funny moustache of his.'

She was right, of course, why would anyone be interested in what I thought? Even so, the prospect of speaking was already starting to give me a headache.

'I suppose we've no time for a cup of tea?' I said, looking towards the kettle and our china cups. I should really get another china cup for when Paul came around, although it was very rare that I had two visitors at the same time.

Mrs Dawson looked at her watch and then at the clock on the kitchen wall. The kitchen clock was ten minutes slow, I really needed to get a new battery. The corner shop sold them ten for 99p which seemed a good deal.

'We really should get off,' she repeated. 'We don't want to miss out on anything.'

We walked down to the nearest bus stop which was two doors along from Patel's. It was a nice and cool morning with a gentle breeze. I wasn't a fan of the hot weather and preferred it a bit chillier.

'I wonder if I should pop in and see that everything is running smoothly,' said Paul, looking over towards his shop.

'We've no time for that,' said Mrs Dawson as

the number 29 pulled up.

The double-decker bus had seen better days. Its red paint was peeling at the front and there was a slight dent in the wing.

'I'll get these,' said Paul as he produced a ten pound note from a leather embossed wallet with the word 'Mumbai' on the front together with a scene showing a mountainous area surrounded by palm trees. It had been a gift for his birthday from a distant aunt still living in India.

The sullen driver eyed us up and down as we got on the bus. He was a large, sweaty, scruffy looking sort of man who looked like the only exercise he got was getting in and out of his cab. Beads of sweat formed on his forehead as well as under his arms, soaking through to his overly tight blue shirt. He had a smell that reminded me of the hamster I'd once had as a small girl. It was a long time ago but I still missed little Reggie. He loved his little wheel, running around it endlessly at night. I couldn't imagine the bus driver ever running anywhere.

'Three returns to the Guildhall, please,' said Paul.

The driver took the ten pound note and gave Paul three tickets without saying anything. He started to pull away before we could even sit down, jostling us slightly to one side.

Mrs Dawson leaned closer towards me.

'I remember when the fare was 2d,' she said. 'Of course, that was a very long time ago and the drivers weren't so surly.'

She said it just loud enough so the driver could hear but there was no reaction. He indeed looked very unhealthy and overweight, almost as if he had been shoe-horned into his cab.

We sat together on a three-seater seat with Paul sat next to me and Mrs Dawson on the end. The seat was quite hard and there was a small hole where part of the stuffing had been pulled out. The back of the seat in front had the words, 'Darren loves Kells,' complete with three kisses, written in black felt-tip pen.

I felt uncomfortable talking to Paul with Mrs Dawson so close, which, of course, was silly. I told her all my business, anyway.

'I wonder if there will be many people there?' I asked.

The bus rattled at it turned left, bouncing us up and down slightly. The suspension had long since given up the ghost. I'm sure that it must have given a smooth ride at one time but that was a long time ago.

'All the boys managed to deliver the leaflets,' said Paul. 'Sanjay wanted to go out again.'

Mrs Dawson smiled as she got comfortable, pushing the seat's innards gently back in the hole they were protruding from.

'It's all a bit late in the day, though,' she said, 'as I'm sure the council realised. A meeting like this needs to be announced long in advance so a strong opposition can be put together.'

As Mrs Dawson was speaking, I was looking at Paul. I suppose he did look something like an Indian Buddy Holly. He caught me looking at him and I gave him a quick smile and then looked away and out of the window at the passing buildings. Many were dirty, soot and exhaust fume covered, and had seen better days. The council no longer had the resources to clean them all.

'Tickets, please,' someone announced from the

aisleway.

I looked up. It was Emo, complete with his wild ginger hair and his grey zip up flying suit. I hadn't noticed how tall he was before. He was well over six feet. His gaze bored into us, he had a wide-eyed vacant look almost as if he was somewhere else. In his head, he probably was.

Mrs Dawson tutted.

'Just ignore him,' she said. 'Pretend you haven't noticed.'

Emo grinned at us inanely. I'm sure that he was probably harmless but at the same time, there was something very threatening about him.

'Tickets please,' he repeated leaning closer towards us. There was an odd smell of garlic. I felt uncomfortable and pretended not to notice him and continued staring out of the window.

Paul fumbled through his pockets and found a crumpled up parking ticket which he gave to Emo.

'Hmm,' said Emo, taking it. 'A return to Portolooe.'

He pretended to clip it with an invisible tool and then handed it back to Paul before heading to the back of the bus where he sat in the middle of the aisle with a wide grin on his face.

'Is there a place called Portolooe?' I asked.

'Isn't that a chemical toilet?' replied Mrs Dawson.

The rest of the journey was pretty uneventful. Emo started to sing 'Show me the way to go home' at one point but soon got off. We avoided eye contact with him as he walked slowly by us.

'I wonder where he lives?' I asked. 'I've only ever seen him on the bus.'

'I think he stays at The Salvation Army Hostel,' Mrs Dawson replied.

I suddenly felt very sorry for him. His life seemed to just involve getting on and off the bus, asking for people's tickets before returning 'home' to the Salvation Army Hostel. I wondered if he had any family or friends and I wondered what he did for the rest of his time. Many treated him as a joke, a source of entertainment, constantly saying 'tickets please', it was no life, was it? I became obsessed with Emo for the rest of the journey, feeling slightly depressed by his lot. It wouldn't take much for any of us to end up like that, I reasoned.

I was brought back to reality by Mrs Dawson ringing the bus's bell.

We got off near to the Guildhall, the grey structure had an imposing, grim feel about it. It was an old building, built some time after the Second World War. Constant traffic had stained the brickwork and the building's combined statues, a charcoaly, sooty black colour. Council workers had, at one time, started to clean the building with power washers but had then abandoned the idea leaving long light streaks up and down the outside. One worker had cleverly written his name, accompanied by a smiley face, in the dirt. I wondered who 'Tommy 2017' was, his artwork forever engraved into the wall, greeting any visitors who passed that way.

As we got closer we could see there were quite a few people collected around the outside of the building, jostling to get a better position to hear anything that might be announced. The nearer we got, it became apparent that all the people there were protesting against the closure of the library. Several had signs

which read, 'Stop the closures - save our libraries.'
Mr Peters appeared at the doorway. He looked slightly
put upon.

'Gemma,' he shouted, waving his hand to get
our attention. 'This way.'
He held the door open with one hand and ushered us in
with the other. As we entered the Guildhall, I could see
that it was quite full with disgruntled readers and other
people annoyed with the council's work.

'There must be over five hundred people here,'
I said. 'All from a few leaflets.'

'This will have thrown the council,' said Mrs
Dawson. 'They were probably expecting just a handful
of objectors.'

'I've saved you some seats,' said Mr Peters,
edging us carefully through the crowd.
I could see all the library staff gathered together. Brian,
with his hand-knitted tank top, Callum with a t-shirt
which read 'Free The Workers,' Miss Moorhouse,
dressed head to foot in tweed, and Miss Taylor dressed
as usual, in black. Mr Peters had a snazzy yellow
waistcoat on.

'Hello, Gemma,' said Miss Taylor,
unexpectedly.

'Hello,' I replied, uncertain what her first name
was.

'It's Dorothy,' she whispered quietly, smiling.
A shiver went up my spine. I hoped that she didn't
think that we were now, somehow, friends. I didn't
mind tolerating her at work but I certainly didn't want
to socialise with her.

Jack Smethurst, the head of the Conservative
council, appeared on stage, to loud jeering and boos. A
man on the stage waved his arms about trying to calm

the baying crowd. Councillor Smethurst was better known as 'Doddy' to most of his constituents. Perhaps it was due to his buck teeth and his mop of dyed, jet black hair. It wasn't a good look.

'We're here today, regrettably,' he said, 'to discuss the closure of the local library.'

'Shame,' shouted one old man from the back of the room. He waved his walking stick high in the air, as high as his arthritic limbs would let him.
Someone started clapping but soon stopped when they realised that no-one else was applauding.

'I'm afraid it's all down to budget cuts,' said Smethurst. 'We just haven't got the money to keep all the smaller libraries going.'

'Nonsense,' a voice piped up from the front. It came from Councillor Evans.

'There is plenty of money,' he continued. 'If I was the head of the council, we wouldn't even be having this discussion.'

'With all respect,' replied Smethurst. 'It was the Labour council that got us into this mess in the first place.'

'Nonsense,' repeated Councillor Evans but said no more.

'He's an overweight idiot,' said Mrs Dawson. 'If we're relying on him to save the library, we might as well go home now.'

'The community needs the library,' someone at the back shouted.

'They'll still have the Central Library,' Smethurst replied.

'Not everyone would find that convenient,' shouted a small, old woman sat near by.
Mr Peters stood up.

'I manage the library,' he said, in a slightly shaky voice. 'The library is essential to local people, those unable to travel further afield easily. It's not just about just lending books, there are information services, community activities, children's groups and a whole range of events run from the building.'

'Hear, hear,' someone shouted loudly from the audience.

Smethurst looked disgruntled towards the audience member.

'I realise all this,' he said, 'but where does the money come from to run these things?'

Councillor Evans got to his feet. His buttoned up white shirt looked particularly tight today.

'From the government,' he shouted.

Councillor Smethurst smiled, half sneering.

'My colleague seems to think that there's an endless pit of money,' he said. 'Well, I'm here to tell you that there isn't.'

'We could have a fundraising event,' suggested Mr Peters.

'That might work in the short term,' said Smethurst, 'but you can't fundraise forever.'

The crowd jeered and booed some more.

A small television team were filming the meeting from the front of the audience. The local press were there also, edging closer to the stage to make sure that they didn't miss anything.

'Just how much would it take to keep the library open?' shouted a reporter.

'I don't know,' replied Councillor Smethurst. 'I haven't got the figures.'

'Thousands? Tens of thousands? Hundreds of thousands?' suggested the reporter.

'Millions,' replied Councillor Smethurst. 'A long term investment would be needed, pouring endless money into a desperate non-profit making organisation.'

'But it would be possible?' asked the reporter.

'It isn't going to happen,' answered Smethurst. 'Now, any more questions?'

'When are the next council elections?' one man shouted.

There was much laughter.

'Not for another year yet,' replied a flustered Councillor Smethurst.

'Well, you can guarantee, I won't be voting for you,' the man in the audience shouted.

There was much jeering and the crowd began getting raucous.

Paul leaned closer to me.

'Perhaps we should leave,' he suggested. 'It looks like a fight might start at any minute.'

A tomato left an audience member's hand and hit Councillor Smethurst straight in the face. There was a loud cheer. I put my arm through Mrs Dawson's arm and whispered, 'I think we should go.'

'I think you're right, dear,' said Mrs Dawson, as more squishy vegetables were thrown in the direction of the stage.

'I hope they're not from Patel's,' said Paul.

We gathered our stuff together as we prepared to leave.

'Wait,' a voice said loudly from the side wings. We turned to look to see where it was coming from and saw Norman Drudge approaching the centre of the stage.

'Wait,' he repeated. 'I have in my hand a piece of paper.'

It was a phrase we'd all heard before.

'He reminds me of Neville Chamberlain,' said Mrs Dawson. 'Him from the Second World War. I suppose we might as well listen to what he has to say.' Someone signalled to the audience to quieten down. When it was reasonably peaceful, Norman spoke again.

'I have in my hand a piece of paper from the Lord Mayor of London,' he said.

'What does it say?' someone shouted from the audience.

Norman glanced down at the letter. He obviously knew it off by heart but fiddled nervously with the piece of paper, his eyes darting back and forwards between it and the audience.

'It says,' continued Norman, 'that after much deliberation, it has been decided that the library won't be closed down after all and that money will be found to keep it open.'

The audience cheered. Councillor Smethurst snatched the piece of paper from Norman so that he could read it himself.

'Good old Norman,' said Mr Peters, turning to me and smiling.

Did Mr Peters really call Gerald Williams 'Norman'?

'Well, that's a turn up for the books,' said Mrs Dawson. 'You'll get to keep your job after all and things will soon be back to normal.'

I wasn't sure if I was happy or sad. While I wanted to keep my job and had enjoyed living on my own at my flat with Mrs Dawson coming around occasionally for tea and to watch an old film, I'd begun to imagine my life married to Paul working in the corner shop. Of course, that's all it was, a dream. I hardly knew Paul apart from a few walks, a trip to the cinema and fish and chips with his family.

The crowd slowly dispersed from the hall.

'Gemma,' Mr Peters shouted. 'We're closing the library tomorrow. A sort of transitioning period. But we'll open again on Thursday. I'll see you bright and early.'

We caught the bus just outside the Guildhall.

'You're strangely quiet,' said Mrs Dawson as we all sat upstairs on the double decker. 'What is it?'

'It's nothing,' I replied, embarrassed to tell Mrs Dawson the reason why.

Emo appeared on the bus again. He'd put some strange gel in his wild, unkempt, curly ginger hair which had the result of flatten down the sides while the rest flopped around on top.

'Tickets, please,' he said.

Paul handed him the same ticket. Emo looked at it and smiled.

'Did you enjoy your trip to Portolooe?' he asked.

'Very much so,' replied Paul.

'Did they save the library?' asked Emo.

I was surprised that he knew anything about the library closure or the meeting at the Guildhall.

'Yes,' said Paul, smiling. It was a kindly smile, not the sneering type that most people gave Emo, especially children and older teenagers.

'Good,' said Emo, without saying any more. He took a seat away from us at the back of the bus and stared out of the window as if he was looking for something or someone.

After two stops, Mrs Dawson got up.

'Where are you going?' I asked.

'I need to get some shopping,' she answered.

225

'But you haven't got your trolley,' I said.

'It's alright, dear,' she said. 'It's just bits.'

She rang the bell for the next stop. She looked at me and then over to Paul.

'Tell him,' she said quietly.

Paul was busy staring out of the window so didn't hear. He turned and waved as Mrs Dawson got off the bus.

'Bye bye, Mrs Dawson,' Emo shouted from the back of the bus.

Paul turned towards me.

'You're very quiet today,' he said. 'Is something bothering you? It's good news that you won't be losing your job, isn't it?'

'Yes, but,' I said.

I bit my bottom lip gently. I had a habit of doing this when I felt uncomfortable.

'What is it?' said Paul.

'You'll laugh if I tell you,' I said.

'I won't laugh,' he said. 'I promise.'

'No, it's nothing,' I said. 'Forget it.'

'Tell me,' said Paul. 'Please.'

'Well,' I said. 'I'd got used to the idea of losing my job. I had a dream, I know it sounds silly, where we got married and I worked in the corner shop.'

Paul smiled.

'Your dream is to work in a corner shop?' he joked. 'It isn't nearly as exciting as the library. It's not all glamour and reduced tins of baked beans, you know.'

'But I'd be with you,' I replied. 'Of course, the whole idea is just a silly dream.'

'I like the idea,' said Paul, smiling.

He grasped hold of my hand and held it all the way back home.

226

Chapter Eighteen

I was still in my pyjamas and drinking a mug of coffee when Mrs Dawson called around at 9am on Wednesday morning. Coffee seemed to wake me up and help me concentrate. The door bell sounded particularly loud this morning. I buzzed her in and she made her way up the stairs to my flat.

'Those steps don't get any easier,' she said, slightly out of breath.
She looked me up and down, observing that I'd not long got out of bed.

'Sorry, dear,' she continued. 'I thought that you would be up by now.'

'I had a lot to think about,' I said, doing my best to straighten my night attire.

'Paul?' she asked.

'Yes,' I replied.' There seems to be so many changes all at once.'

'Isn't that a good thing?' Mrs Dawson asked.

'I suppose so,' I said, 'it's just so much has been happening over the last couple of weeks. I'll probably get back to normal when I return to work tomorrow.' Mrs Dawson looked over to the kitchen and the pile of dishes in the sink, left untouched from the night before. It wasn't like me to leave everything unwashed, waiting for them to be cleaned the next day. I liked everything tidy before I went to bed. Dishes washed and put back in the cupboard, clothes put in the washing machine and books and magazines tidied away on their shelves.

'What do you plan to do today?' Mrs Dawson asked. 'It's nice and sunny out.'

I gazed out through the kitchen window towards the street. The rays of the sun were reflecting on the yellow vinyl topped table. The table had been an early charity shop buy. I think that it dated back to the 1960s. I wondered how many people had eaten around it before I'd bought it. It was full of character and was another piece of furniture, besides my comfy armchair, that I could never part with.

'I might see if there's an old film on,' I said but realised that I probably wouldn't be able to concentrate. Mrs Dawson looked at me in a concerned sort of way. I straightened my dressing gown suddenly feeling very untidy.

'You get dressed,' she said, 'and I'll wash the dishes and make you some breakfast and perhaps we could go for a walk around the park. The fresh air will clear your head.'

'Oh, you don't have to do that,' I said, half protesting.

Mrs Dawson smiled and edged me gently in the direction of the bathroom.

'It's fine, dear,' she said. 'I'm happy to help.'

My blackbird was back, his feathers slightly ruffled, singing away and tapping on the kitchen window, his bright yellow beak making a rat-a-tat-tat noise against the glass.

'There's Alf,' said Mrs Dawson, smiling. 'All's well that ends well. That's what he used to say. Alf, that is.'

Mrs Dawson did make a wonderful breakfast, not a breakfast I would usually cook myself. There was something lovely about someone else making it for me. I couldn't remember the last time someone had made my breakfast. Sausages, bacon and eggs and toast with butter and marmalade on, proper marmalade that it, not any of that cheap stuff, and piping hot tea in a china cup.

'You spoil me,' I said as I tucked in.

'Well, I never get to cook for anyone nowadays,' said Mrs Dawson. 'Not since Alf has been gone. Is it okay?'

'It's lovely,' I replied. 'Probably the best breakfast I've had in a long time.'
I wondered what life would be like if Mrs Dawson moved in? A surrogate sort of mother who gave me advice and cooked me breakfast. Perhaps I was incapable of living a normal life on my own although I certainly wasn't going to suggest the idea to her. I'm sure that she had much better things to do than chase around after me.

By 10.30am, we were sat by the duck pond. The randy duck made himself known by quacking and tapping hard on my foot. Again, I didn't have any bread for him. He sort of looked angry, if a duck could look angry. He certainly quacked more aggressively than usual.

'Didn't you want to see Paul this morning?' asked Mrs Dawson.

'No,' I replied. 'Well, yes, I did but I'm not sure how I should behave, what I should say.'

'Just let it come naturally,' replied Mrs Dawson. 'Alf and I were stepping out for six months before he picked up the courage to kiss me. And then it was on the forehead. He was a lot taller than me.'

'Oh,' I said.

The duck quacked some more before giving up and returning to the pond.

'That was good news about the library,' said Mrs Dawson. 'I think that even Miss Moorhouse cracked a smile.'

'Yes,' I said, 'and Miss Taylor called me Gemma.'

'Whatever next?' Mrs Dawson joked.

There was a few seconds silence as the randy duck returned and once again pecked my shoe before clearing off to find someone who had actually gone to the trouble to bring him some bread.

'What about Mr Raman?' I said. 'Will you be seeing him again.'

'Oh, yes,' replied Mrs Dawson. 'Seeing you and Paul together made me realise that we shouldn't pass up any chance that comes our way. And I'm not getting any younger.'

'It's just...,' I began.

'Yes, dear?' said Mrs Dawson.

'It's just that I don't want anything to change,' I continued. 'I like our Thursday morning cups of tea, watching old films on the sofa, meeting at the charity shop and library, going to the park.'

'Nothing has to change, dear,' said Mrs Dawson. 'We can still do all that.'

'But you'll be off with Mr Raman, I'll be with

Paul,' I said. 'And then there's Paul's family, his mother, his father, his aunties, little Sanjay and all their relatives. Everything will change unless I continue my life exactly as it is now.'

'Oh, you don't want to do that,' said Mrs Dawson. 'Live your life. Nothing will change. We'll see each other just as much.'

I realised I saw Mrs Dawson as the grandmother I never had. I couldn't bear to lose her. And I liked normality, where I knew what every day held. Change just made me feel, well, anxious. I wanted to leave Winslow Place every morning, with its old grey slate paving stones, pass Mr Bishop cleaning his car, say good morning to Mr Graves, be ignored by Mrs Graves, walk along the tree lined lanes of Rennie Avenue, along Marsh Road with its dilapidated terraced houses, up Cornwall Street and up towards Portland Road where the library was based. I wanted Thursdays off when Mrs Dawson and me would sip the best tea from our favourite china cups while putting the world to rights. I wanted to walk around the duck pond feeding the birds scraps of bread. I wanted to work in the charity shop on Saturday mornings and have a natter with Mrs Walters. I wanted to see my friendly blackbird at the window every morning as I ate my breakfast. I wanted to look across and see Norman Drudge, Gerald, drinking tea and eating biscuits. I wanted to pop into the corner shop and get my groceries from Patel's while talking about the weather or the state of the pavements. I just wanted life to be as normal as it could be, to continue as it was.

Only things had changed and life would never be the same again. I could feel a headache coming on.

'Nothing has to change,' Mrs Dawson repeated.

Unable to find anything to eat, the randy duck came back, quacked and stared at us. It was a stare that seemed to say, 'You've let me down.'

'I wish we'd brought some bread,' said Mrs Dawson. 'This little chap is hungry.'

We stared at the small duck and he quacked some more.

'Norman came good in the end,' I said.

'Yes,' said Mrs Dawson, 'Who would have thought that little quiet man from across the way would save the day.'

'I should talk to him more,' I said. 'Perhaps I'll even call him Gerald. It somehow doesn't seem right calling him Norman Drudge anymore.'

'I suppose not, said Mrs Dawson. 'Although Norman does suit him better. How old is he?'

'Fifty five, perhaps?' I answered.

'And no partner?' said Mrs Dawson. 'How old is Mrs Walters in the charity shop?'

'Sixties?' I suggested.

'Perhaps we could match them up,' said Mrs Dawson.

'Oh, I don't know,' I said. 'I think that she may be too old for him.'

I struggled to see long-term bachelor Norman Drudge with homely Mrs Walters.

'Just a thought,' said Mrs Dawson.

She reached into her handbag and pulled out a packet of Polo mints. She offered me one which I accepted. I whispered a quiet 'thank you'.

'I read Rebecca,' I said. 'It was wonderful. When Mrs Danvers burned down Mandalay, I imagined a similar thing happening to the library but involving Miss Taylor.'

Mrs Dawson laughed.

'Will you see Paul today?' she asked.

'I'm popping into the shop later,' I replied. 'I've bought Sanjay one of those high-powered water pistols to thank him for delivering the leaflets.'

'Oh dear,' said Mrs Dawson. 'It will only lead to mischief.'

'I suppose I should have bought them all one,' I said. 'All the children, that is. They're so expensive, though. I suppose he can share it.'

We sat staring at the pond for a while before Mrs Dawson returned home at 11.30am to do some 'spring cleaning'.

I decided to return to the park in the afternoon and, this time, take some bread. I walked over to Patel's just after 1pm. Paul was busy arranging vegetables outside in home-made wooden boxes. There was a special offer on cauliflowers.

'I was going to come over later,' said Paul. 'I just need to get someone to cover for the shop. Mr and Mrs Patel have gone into town. Mr Patel needs a new suit, apparently. He never goes anywhere to wear it.'

It seemed odd Paul calling his parents Mr and Mrs Patel.

'Mrs Dawson is seeing Mr Raman again,' I said.

'Good,' replied Paul. 'They're well-matched.'

He took some carrots out of a sealed polythene bag and spread them around the cauliflower before placing a card in the shape of a star beside them. It had 'reduced' written on it in felt-tip pen.

'She still loves Alf,' I said. 'I think they'll just be friends. I can't see Mrs Dawson ever marrying again.'

Paul looked down towards the odd-shaped carrier under

my arm.

'What's in the bag?' he asked.

I lifted out the super-powered water pistol. It looked a lot larger than it had done in the shop. It had a pump-action jet spray attachment on the top. I wondered if I should have just bought him a toy car or something else less aggressive.

'It's for Sanjay,' I said. 'It's to thank him for delivering the leaflets.'

Paul smiled.

'Oh, dear,' he said. 'We had better keep out of his way once you give him this.'

He held it up and pretended to shoot a pigeon off Mr Graves' top guttering. I imagined him shooting Miss Graves with it as she walked by. I wondered what her reaction might be.

'Do you fancy a walk around the allotments later?' Paul continued. 'After work, at about 5pm? It looks like it's going to be a lovely evening.'

He put the water pistol back in its bag and rolled it up tightly as if he was trying to conceal it from someone.

'That would be lovely,' I said.

'And perhaps you could come for tea afterwards?' he said. 'Brinda, Chandra and Devyani keep asking me when they are going to see you again.'

'I'd love to,' I said, feeling more confident than I had when I first went to the Patels for tea.

'And no fish and chips,' joked Paul.

I smiled.

'Where are you off to now?' he continued.

'Just a walk around the park,' I said. 'Feed the hungry birds and think about things. It helps me relax.'

'Oh,' said Paul.

He disappeared into the shop and came back with a loaf

of bread.

'For the ducks,' he said. 'It's on special offer, two for 59p. It's free to you, of course.'

'Thanks,' I whispered and wandered off, happy, towards the park.

It was quiet when I arrived but the ducks were glad to see me, especially the randy one. It seemed odd that he actually recognised me but perhaps he just saw me as another person with a loaf of bread.

The afternoon was pretty lonely, just me and the ducks. I thought that I might have bumped into Mrs Dawson again but she was nowhere to be seen. There were many joggers about, running circuits of the park, oblivious to anyone, or anything, that got in their way. Their rudeness knew no bounds and I watched as the old, disabled and just about everyone else jumped quickly out of their way to avoid being knocked over. It was worse when there was a crowd of them. The Parkside Runners were particularly notorious for their aggressive behaviour towards normal pedestrians.

'They shouldn't be allowed in the park,' Mrs Dawson said often. 'Or anywhere else, for that matter.' Of course, they were second only to cyclists. Not the normal, take it easy, cyclists but the ones who raced about at speed, swearing at people as they passed them and nearly ran them over.

'Mrs Bromley's labradoodle lost it's leg after being in collision with a cyclist,' Mrs Dawson told me. 'And the cyclist had the cheek to blame the dog.' It was all getting too busy for me and, without Mrs Dawson for company, I decided to return home.

Paul called around for me just after 5pm. It was a clear, crisp evening. It was nice to see someone and I was looking forward to our evening walk around the allotments.

'Sanjay was pleased with his water pistol,' said Paul. 'You'll probably see him at the allotments, he wanted to try it out.'

'I hope he's not firing it at small animals or birds,' I said. 'Maybe I shouldn't have bought it for him. I wouldn't want him getting in trouble again.'

'Oh, no. I think he learned his lesson after the firework incident,' said Paul.

The allotments were quite busy with people tending to their vegetables and others just out for an evening stroll. Old fence panels had been placed against the wall, ready to be broken up to be burned on an already large and smokey bonfire. The smoke billowed towards the old houses at Duberry Street. I wondered if their washing was still out, strung out on lines to dry in the evening sun, and ending up being covered with smokey deposits. It was the city, they probably all used tumble driers anyway, I assumed.

'Will you come around for tea again on Sunday?' asked Paul.

My mind left the concerns of the residents of Duberry Street's bed sheets and other attire.

'Of course,' I said.

'And we could go to the cinema afterwards?' he said. 'You could choose the film, perhaps?'

'That would be lovely,' I replied. 'Something without so much action, maybe? Certainly no dinosaurs.'

We sat on the bench looking towards the city. Two familiar figures could be seen in the distance, it was Mrs Dawson and Mr Raman. They looked very happy together.

'Hello, dear,' said Mrs Dawson. 'Fancy seeing

you two here.'

She knew quite well that I was going to the allotments with Paul because I had told her earlier. She winked.

'It's a lovely evening,' she said. 'The man on the news forecast rain. I'm not sure they know anymore than we do.'

I smiled.

'We've just passed Norman, by the way,' she continued. 'Looking for dormice.'

'Oh,' I said. 'I hope you didn't call him Norman.

'I nearly did,' said Mrs Dawson. 'But I managed to call him Gerald for the first time.'

'Good,' I said. 'We shouldn't call him Norman Drudge any more.'

'He said that he's going to run for head of the council,' said Mrs Dawson. 'He'll have my vote. Better than that Jack Smethurst or Councillor Evans for that matter.'

I stared out across the fields. There was a slight breeze gently blowing through the long grass.

'Back to the library tomorrow,' I said. 'I wonder if anything will have changed?'

I knew that it wouldn't have but I felt apprehensive all the same. I was sure that Mr Peters would still have his ornate moustache, Miss Moorhouse would still be frosty towards everyone, Brian would have on his nerdy tank top, Callum would be busily rearranging the children's section and Miss Taylor, well, who knew what Miss Taylor would be like.

'Gemma's coming for tea on Sunday,' said Paul. 'Would you and Mr Raman like to come also?'

I was hoping Mrs Dawson would say 'yes' as I felt far less uncomfortable with her around.

'Won't it be a bit, well, busy?' asked Mrs

Dawson. 'We wouldn't want to put your mother out.'

'She'd be pleased to see you,' said Paul. 'The more the merrier.'

'Well, thank you, that's very kind of you,' said Mrs Dawson. 'We would be happy to attend.'

We all realised that she hadn't asked Mr Raman if he wanted to go but he looked quite happy with the situation and smiled and nodded towards Paul.

We sat on the bench watching the sun slowly set. The sky turned a beautiful shade of orange, silhouetting the sheds, bean poles and people attending their allotments against the fiery heavens.

'Beautiful,' said Mr Raman. 'Have you ever seen anything so wondrous?'

Gerald Williams could be seen in the distance foraging through the long grass. He had a small camera as well as a notepad and pen busily recording the activities of the dormice.

The sound of spades turning over soil and the constant chirping of grasshoppers could be heard. A crow cawed loudly in the distance. A bonfire crackled with heavy, white smoke billowing up into the sky as an allotment holder burned grass and other discarded rubbish.

Mrs Dawson reached into her bag and pulled out a tartan thermos flask. She was always prepared for every occasion.

'Cup of tea anyone?' she asked.

I hadn't imagined Mrs Dawson drinking tea out of a thermos flask especially after our Thursday morning ritual of always drinking tea from a warmed teapot with proper tea served in china cups and saucers.

For that moment in time, everything seemed perfect. It was a beautiful evening. Everyone that I cared about were all in one place. I hadn't lost my job, Mrs Dawson

was stepping out with Mr Raman and I had Paul.
A lone pigeon flew overhead. As I looked up, it pooped right on me.

'Oh dear,' said Mrs Dawson, as she handed me her handkerchief, the one with the embroidered initials in the corner.

'It's supposed to be lucky,' she said, 'being pooped on by a bird.'

'I do feel lucky,' I said as I wiped it away.
I felt guilty that I'd made such a mess of Mrs Dawson's fancy handkerchief.

'Don't worry,' she said. 'It will wash.'

It had been an odd couple of weeks but everything that had happened over the last fortnight had brought my life into some sort of prospective. Even with bird's mess on me, I was happier than I had been in a long time.

'Oh to be in England, now that spring is here,' said Mr Raman, slightly misquoting Robert Browning. I realised in that split second the importance of libraries, community and friendship.

As we sat watching the sun go down for that brief half an hour, I felt that all was perfect with the world and things could only get better.
Mrs Dawson smiled over at me.

'It never did rain,' she said.

About the author

Iain Dalgleish was born in Edinburgh in 1968 and now lives in sunny Cornwall. His books include *The Ups and Downs of Norman Drudge*, *God Save the Queen* and *The Minion*.

He can be contacted at iaindalgleishauthor@gmail.com

Printed in Great Britain
by Amazon

38758057R00144